A Kingpin's Dynasty 2

D1712834

Tina J

Copyright 2018

More Books by Tina J

A Thin Line Between Me & My Thug 1-2
I Got Luv for My Shawty 1-2
Kharis and Caleb: A Different kind of Love 1-2
Loving You is a Battle 1-3
Violet and the Connect 1-3
You Complete Me
Love Will Lead You Back
This Thing Called Love
Are We in This Together 1-3
Shawty Down to Ride For a Boss 1-3
When a Boss Falls in Love 1-3
Let Me Be The One 1-2
We Got That Forever Love
Ain't No Savage Like The One I got 1-2
A Queen & Hustla 1-2 (collab)
Thirsty for a Bad Boy 1-2
Hasaan and Serena: An Unforgettable Love 1-2
We Both End Up With Scars
Caught up Luvin a beast 1-3
A Street King & his Shawty 1-2
I Fell for the Wrong Bad Boy 1-2 (collab)
Addicted to Loving a Boss 1-3
All Eyes on the Crown 1-3
I Need that Gangsta Love 1-2 (collab)
Still Luvin' a Beast 1-2
Creepin' With The Plug 1-2
I Wanna Love You 1-2
Her Man, His Savage 1-2
When She's Bad, I'm Badder 1-3
Marco & Rakia 1-3
Feenin' for a Real One 1-3
A Kingpin's Dynasty 1-3

Previously...

Dynasty

I watched Menace walk out the door and went straight to the Uber app on my phone. He didn't have to tell me but I knew something was wrong with Taylor. After I put it in to come get me, I threw my clothes on and called Jen. She was still recuperating from giving birth and in a lotta pain. The doctor gave her eight stiches in her private area because the tear was bad. She said it was even more painful trying to use the bathroom. Shit, hearing all that, I don't even know if I want kids.

"Hey girl." She answered and sounded a little groggy

"Hey. Did Valley leave?"

"Yea. Menace called and said something happened."

"I knew it."

"Knew what?" I started explaining everything and she agree something was wrong.

"Well, I know when they do find the guy, he's gonna wish he never laid eyes on her. Joakim is gonna lose his mind if anything happens to her."

"Jen, if she loses the baby."

"I don't even wanna think about it."

"Me either. Let me call you back."

"Where you going Dy?"

"To the store. Menace left me here and there's nothing to cook and before you say anything, I'll be fine. Its not far from his house." I closed the door and hopped in the car.

"Dynasty, I think you should wait and let him take you."

"Too late. I'm in the Uber."

"What store are you going to?" I told her which one and she refused to hang the phone up until I got back home. I placed the Bluetooth in my ear and grabbed a shopping cart.

"You better make him a hearty meal because when he finds out you left, he'll be mad, fuck the shit outta you and then wanna eat." I busted out laughing.

I stayed in the store for almost an hour buying tons of food and snacks. I did know how to cook before I went to jail and I've been doing a lot of it, in my new place. My mom always tried to but I wanted her to see, I remembered what she taught me. I had been on you tube watching videos on Iheart recipes too. That woman made a lot of southern food and I found myself trying out, a lot of it. By the time I finished and the lady bagged my items, I had spent over two hundred dollars.

"Hold on Jen, while I put in for a ride to pick me up." With this new iPhone, I could talk and still browse the internet.

"Ok, I'm back." I stood in the vestibule of the store and continued talking to her.

"You're a hard person to find." I turned around and Block was standing there with a dumb grin on his face.

"What do you want?"

"Who is that Dynasty? Never mind, don't answer and keep me on the phone. I'm calling Valley on the house phone."

"What do you want Block?"

"Oh shit. Fuck!" I could hear Jen yelling in the background.

"How the hell are you fucking my boss? Then you let him beat my ass and didn't even come to see if I was ok." The Uber pulled up and it was the same guy who dropped me off. He got out and started helping me put the bags in the car.

"Block, I messed around with Menace before I even knew you." I could see he confusion on his face.

"As far as, him fighting you, he saw you beating on me. What did you expect?"

"I can't reach anyone Dynasty. Hurry up and get in the car." I heard Jen yelling in my ear and Lord knows, I was trying and I think the guy was too. He was rushing to take the bags out the cart.

"So, you just fucking the crew?"

"Block, you and I could've been together but you had a hand problem and I'll be damned if I go through the same thing with another man."

"The same thing."

"I dealt with a man in the past who.-" I stopped myself when I saw her.

"Who what?" I watched her walk closer to me with a smirk on her face and the bag of eggs in my hand, dropped.

"Is that? Is that?" I couldn't believe my eyes.

"Block, why are you conversing with the bitch who killed your cousin?" He turned to me and I can't tell you what happened because with the blow on the back of my head, everything went black.

Block

"What the fuck is wrong with you?" I barked at Ruthie as we ran to the car.

"What?"

"Ruthie, you have your son here; my cousin and if anything happened to him because of the bullshit you just pulled, your ass would've been on the ground next to her."

"Oh, so its ok she killed your cousin; my man?" I looked in the rearview mirror and saw cop cars and an ambulance pulling up.

Just as Ruthie told me Dynasty is the one who killed my cousin, she hit her in the head with the butt of the gun. That wasn't as bad as hearing Dynasty's head hit the ground. The way it bounced off the pavement was even worse. I picked my little cousin up and ran. Luckily, he had some beats on and he was looking down on the Nintendo switch he was playing. He didn't need to see no shit like that. Hell, I didn't wanna see it.

"From what my aunt told me, he wasn't your man." She sucked her teeth.

I was young when my cousin was murdered by his girlfriend. I never knew who the chick was and to this day, I still didn't until she blurted it out. Whenever, I asked my aunt she'd say it doesn't matter and that had she been in the same situation, she would've done the same. I was pissed but after she told me everything he did to the woman, I could understand. In my mind and Quana's, she didn't have to kill him though. I guess we can't really say what we'd do unless it was us.

Quana on the other hand hated the chick who did it. She also, never said her name. When I asked why, she said the bitch didn't need to get any exposure for taking her best friend away. Her and Jamal supposedly were very close, which is how she knew about the baby. Evidently, Ruthie was best friends with Dynasty and sleeping with him behind her back. She popped up pregnant and he told her to get rid of it and as you can see, she didn't. From the reaction on Dynasty's face, Ruthie never told her. Now I see, why Ruthie slept with me and wanted to get her back. She was in love with my cousin and felt Dynasty was in the way. All she wants now is to destroy Dynasty, which is crazy when she had no idea any of it was going on. This is the exact reason I say, *bitches ain't shit.*

"He wasn't hers, if he were sleeping with me." She smirked and I laughed.

"So you believe you're the only one he cheated on her with? You can't be that stupid." That smirk left her face.

"Whatever. Where we going?"

"Bitch, I'm dropping you off." I parked in front of her house and the shit was taped off.

"What happened here?"

"Oh, my mom wouldn't give me any money so I stabbed her. Lets go somewhere else." She looked down at her phone.

"WHAT?"

"You heard me. I gave her some money and told her to keep it for my son's future. When I asked for it back she said no, so she had to go." I looked in the backseat and J.J was still on that game.

"We can't go to my house because I'm sure Menace sent a crew there for me. I can go stay with my aunt but you can't come."

"Where am I supposed to go?"

"I don't know. Quana definitely won't tell where I'm at but with you, that's a different story."

"I thought we were gonna set Menace up."

"We are but I can't do it right now."

"Why not?"

"Because if you're saying they're a couple, he's gonna be looking for us. We have to stay out the spotlight for a little while. He has to think we're nowhere around. Otherwise; he'll come full force and we'll be dead."

"Shit. Ok. Give me some money and I'll go away for a few weeks and we can update one another."

"STAY AWAY RUTHIE!" I yelled and handed her a few thousand dollars. I wasn't making as much money as before and I'm sure, my job is finished so I had to be careful with spending.

"I am. Drop me off at the train station and take my son to your aunt. She'll be happy he can stay there." I parked at the station and waited for her to say goodbye to her son. Unfortunately, she got out and kept it moving. He asked was she coming back and I told him, yes. The only thing is, I didn't know if she was and if she did, if her life would be taken or not.

I went to my aunts' house and drove around the block a few times to make sure no one was watching. I called Quana and told her to open the door.

"What the fuck is going on? Menace, called looking for you and Ruthie." She looked behind me. Jamal went to the back room with my aunt.

"Man, Ruthie fucked up." I started telling her what happened and she shook her head.

"What are you gonna do?"

"Keep my ass in the house until I come up with a plan to get him."

"Block, I'm pissed at Menace for leaving me but what you're tryna do, is suicide."

"Quana, he beat my ass and don't forget he sicked that damn dog on me and my leg ain't been right ever since. When Dynasty gets up, she's gonna tell him who did it. You don't think he'll come after me?"

"Maybe, if I talk to him." I gave her the side eye.

"What?"

"He don't even fuck with you."

"So."

"So, he won't give two shits about what you have to say. Leave it alone and let me come up with something."

"Block, I don't wanna lose another family member."

"Then help me get him. You know a lot more than I do." I could see her thinking about it and after another ten minutes, she agreed. She said if Ruthie was involved, she wouldn't. I was fine with that because that bitch seemed shady and I can see her messing shit up anyway. I'm just gonna sit back and come up with a plan that won't backfire and will end his life.

Dynasty

"Are you ok?" I opened my eyes and saw Jen, my mom and her boyfriend.

"Where am I?" I tried to sit up and my mom told me to stay put. She pressed the nurses button and sat next to me.

"Honey, do you remember what happened?"

"I was on the phone with Jen, arguing with Block when Ruthie walked up." I gasped and covered my mouth with both hands.

"What's wrong?" I felt the tears rolling down my face.

"Ma, she is the one Jamal had a child with."

"What?"

"She had a little boy with her and ma, he is the exact replica of Jamal. How could they do that to me? I mean, I knew he was cheating but never in a million years would I even assume it was with her."

"Is everything ok?" A nurse came in smiling.

"How long have I been here? Matter of fact, how did I get here?"

"You've been here for a few hours. I'm going to let the doctor know you're awake." She said and walked out.

"The Uber guy must've known you were on the phone and told me what went down." Jen stood in front of me.

"Jen, you didn't have to come. I know you're in a lot of pain."

"Nonsense. Valley's mom came and she was more than happy to keep the baby. You know she thinks he's hers anyway."

"Where's Menace? Is Taylor ok?"

"Honey, I couldn't reach them."

"What you mean?"

"When the guy told me what happened, I immediately got dressed and came. I left my phone at home. I tried to call Valley from here but he didn't answer. His mom is going to tell him where we are. You know, he'll tell Menace." I nodded.

"How are you Ms. Sutton? You had a pretty bad fall." The doctor walked in and started to do some tests. He asked if I remembered what happened, can I feel him touch certain areas and other stuff they do.

"Ok, so you're out of the woods for any brain damage but there is some swelling, due to the fall. You have a few stitches in the back and will suffer headaches. You may suffer short term memory loss and the baby seems to be doing fine."

"BABY!!!!" All three of us shouted out at the same time. I could see my mom's boyfriend Glenn shaking his head. I know, its because he kept hearing my mom say I was.

"Yea. You're about four weeks."

"Four weeks?" I kept questioning him as if his statement would change.

"I told you. Oh my God! I'm gonna be a grandmother."

"I'm the baby's Godmother and you better not even think about giving me and Taylor the positon to share. She's the aunt."

"Wait! How am I pregnant? All the test I took were negative and trust me, it was a lot."

"Do you know how many women come in asking the same question?" I looked at him.

"A lot. For future reference, any time you think it's a possibly you're pregnant and you take a store brought test;

17

always come for a blood test or have a doctor do an ultrasound." I sucked my teeth because Menace said something similar.

"Do you have any questions?"

"No. Can I go home?"

"I want to keep you overnight and if everything is fine, you can leave in the morning." He checked my eyes and throat again and said he'd see me tomorrow.

"SHIT DY. YOU OK? WHAT THE FUCK HAPPENED?" Menace came barging in with Valley behind him.

"I'm ok. Where's Taylor?" I could tell by his facial expression that either, he hadn't found her yet or something bad happened.

"I was right Menace. She's.-"

"Ma, not right now. He doesn't care about that." I cut her off. Both her and Jen looked at me.

"She's what?"

"Nothing. The doctor said I may suffer a little memory loss but its ok. What's the status on Taylor?"

18

"That guy has her. Did she ever mention where he lived?"

"She told me they spent the weekend in New York and that he told her about a place he had in Elizabeth."

"Call Joakim and tell him." He told Valley who walked out.

"Can y'all give us a minute?" He asked and they all stepped out. He sat next to me and pecked my lips.

"Tell me what happened?" I gave him the story and after he yelled at me for leaving the house, he laid next to me.

"Dy, I'm gonna have Valley stay here with you until I get back."

"Menace."

"Once we have Taylor, I want you to stay with me."

"Don't you think its too soon?"

"Not at all. Especially; when I'm tryna get you pregnant. How can I do that when we have to be quiet at your house? I love hearing you moan loud and we can do more freaky shit at my place."

19

"Like what? We already do a bunch of nasty things to one another."

"Yea but I can't fuck you outside. I can't lean you over the stairs and.-"

"Ok. Ok, I get it." I laughed.

"Let me talk to my mom."

"For?"

"I've been away for a while Menace and she may not want me to leave."

"Yea. Yea. Look." He got up after he read a text on his phone.

"Joakim is downstairs waiting on me. You'll be here until tomorrow and Valley will be here. If you need to talk to me, just call."

"Menace be careful."

"I will. Gimme a kiss." I put my arms around his neck.

"Now my dick hard. Fix it."

"What you need me to do?" I slid my hands in his pants and he put his face in the crook of my neck.

"Shit Dy." I could feel him getting harder.

20

"Y'all done talking?" Jen came in and turned back around. He stood up and I pointed at his jeans.

"Fuck Dynasty. How the hell am I supposed to leave with my dick this hard?" He ran in the bathroom and I busted out laughing. A few minutes later everyone came back in and he came out looking guilty as hell.

"I'll see you later and you're gonna finish what you started."

"You damn right I am. And you're gonna do something for me."

"You already know. Get some sleep." He kissed my forehead and took Valley in the hallway with him.

"What the hell were y'all doing?" Jen sat next to me.

"Nothing." I had a grin on my face. I asked my mom to help me in the bathroom to wash up. I asked Jen if she could get housekeeping in to change the sheets. I only had the hospital gown to put on but at least it'll be clean and so will I. My mother closed the door, started the shower, put the toilet seat down and waited for me to get in.

"Why don't you want him to know?"

21

"Ma, he's worried about his sister. I want him to be focused on getting her and not worry about me."

"Are you sure that's it?" I pulled the curtain back.

"Yes, that's why? Why you ask?"

"I'm making sure you're not trying to get rid of it."

"Ma, I may not be ready for a kid but I would never do that. We weren't careful and knew the risk. The baby didn't ask to be here so why terminate it for my mistake?"

"Good because I already picked out a crib for my place."

"Your place?" I started washing up.

"Menace, is gonna want you to move in with him soon, so I may as well set the baby's room up."

"You wouldn't be upset, if I moved out?" She came over to the shower and opened the curtain a little.

"Dynasty, you are a grown woman and if you wanted to move halfway around the world, I'd still support you."

"But…"

"Honey, if you're falling for him and about to have his children, you should move in with him. Or at least stay there more than once a week. He's not about to let you leave him."

"Why is that?"

"Dynasty, I can see how much you two are into each other. All of us can and we all know love is coming soon. You may as well get used to being his one and only now." I smiled listening to her say all those things. Was I in love with him? Wasn't it too soon? What about his ex? Did I feel like going through the same thing Taylor was? I had a lot going on in my head and started getting a headache.

She helped me out and I put on the lotion she had in her purse and two gowns on. I had her press the button for the nurse and ask for some medicine to get rid of this headache. All they could give me was Tylenol but it was something. I laid down and my eyes began to close.

****

"You hungry?" Menace asked.

"When did you get here?" I tried to sit up.

"About an hour ago."

23

"What time is it?"

"Nine thirty. The doctor said you can leave whenever you want."

"I must've slept all night."

"You did. I brought you up a breakfast sandwich and orange juice. I'm gonna heat it up in their small kitchen down the hall."

"Can you have the nurse come in first. I wanna shower and get ready to go." He did what I asked and went to heat the food up. I could've had him assist but we most likely would've done nasty things in there. He loved to hear me moan and I felt the same when it came to him so it was best he didn't.

I came out and he was sitting on the chair smiling. It could be because he brought me an outfit that was tight as hell and he loved seeing my curves. The nurse began reading the discharge papers and what to do if it's an emergency. You know the protocol shit they have to mention before you leave, so the patient doesn't sue. I signed and waited for her to grab a wheelchair. Another thing they had to do.

"I'm tearing that pussy up when we get home." He stood behind me and whispered in my ear.

"You're nasty." I turned around and faced him. He placed his baseball cap on my head and slowly covered my bandage.

"You have no idea, how nasty I'm gonna be."

"Ok. You ready?" I couldn't respond but my kitty sure did. Her ass was wet and ready. I guess, staying with him won't be so bad.

Taylor

"Donnell, please take me back to my truck."

"Where do you think I'm taking you?" The two blows

to my face made me shut right up. I didn't say anything and

stared out the window as he drove.

After he rushed me out the restaurant, he took me to the

hospital and rushed me outta there too. He yelled at the doctor

and told him we had a sick kid at home and he needed to hurry

up and put the stitches in. The entire time we were in there, all

he kept talking about was getting Joakim. Its like he had some

personal vendetta against him and if he did, why not just go

after him. It's like he wanted to torture me for some reason. I

say torture because my hand required twenty stitches, he

punched me in the face twice and he was now driving like a

speed demon. I wanted to ask him to slow down but was scared

of the repercussions. When we pulled up on the side of the

restaurant he stopped short and my face hit the dashboard.

Blood rushed out my nose, instantly.

"Look at the mess you made. CLEAN IT UP!" He tossed paper napkins at me from outta his glove compartment. I had to hold my nose with one hand and clean with the other.

"My truck isn't here. Where is it?" He had a devious grin on his face.

"It means, they know something happened to you. Get out."

"Why are you letting me go?"

"Because I have plans for you and that punk nigga you with." I looked at him and the facial expression he had was one I've never seen. It was like a happy, sad, and angry face all in one.

"Donnell, just take me to the hospital. My nose needs to be checked."

"Did you hear what the fuck I said? Get out and if you mention one word to where I may or may not be, I'm gonna catch your stupid ass slipping again and kill you. Now don't make me say it again." This time he came around to my side, yanked my arm and tossed me on the ground.

"ASSHOLE!" Some lady yelled out.

27

"Are you ok?" She attempted to help me up and I yelled out.

"I think my ankle is twisted." My hand was already wrapped and I could see blood seeping through. I must've busted some stitches.

"Do you need a ride?"

"Can you take me to the hospital?" I asked the woman and she was more than willing.

When I arrived, the receptionist came straight to me and asked if I were ok. She also told me, some men were there looking for me and had just missed me. I described Menace and she claimed it wasn't him. Once I described Joakim she smiled and said that he was the one. If it was him then Menace must've been one of the guys outside. Those two are always together and once Joakim told him something was up, I'm sure he came.

"Let's get your foot checked and I can call someone to pick you up." I nodded, thanked the lady who gave me a ride and asked for her phone number. I planned on calling her tomorrow to get her address and send a thank you gift.

After I finished being seen. I indeed had a sprain in my ankle. They put a small air cast on my foot and had me on crutches. My nose was swollen and I had a black eye. Otherwise; I was good but when my mom saw me, she was pissed off and happy to see I was safe. She pulled the car around and started cursing my brother out to me, for not telling her. I asked her to take me home because I wanted to take a bath and relax. I had a very stressful day. She insisted on staying with me and I was fine with that.

My mom helped me shower, brought me food to eat and stayed in the room with me until I fell asleep. It wasn't until I felt the bed dip and smelled his cologne, did I wake up. He was staring at me and moving my hair out my face. I guess the light from the television made the black eye visible because his entire facial expression changed when he saw it. I moved closer to him and put my head against his chest. I wanted to be as close to him, as possible. I needed to feel safe and secure and he was the only one, able to help me with it. His arms wrapped around my body and I fell straight to sleep.

****

"Nah, she's good." I turned over and saw Joakim standing by the window speaking on the phone. I sat up, grabbed my crutches and walked to the bathroom. I didn't really need them but used them anyway. When I finished, I took the air cast off and placed a plastic bag on my hand to keep it from getting wet and hopped in the shower.

"I'm gonna kill him." He stood behind me in the shower and put his hands on my stomach.

"I was going to tell you that day at the hospital." He kissed the side of my neck.

"Joa, I don't wanna be without you anymore. I'm sorry for being a spoiled brat and seeking revenge." He wiped the tears falling from my eyes. *How the hell did he know I was crying and the shower is on?*

"I deserved it Tay."

"No you didn't. We weren't together and like my mom said, I shouldn't have been mad in the first place. Baby, if you still want me, I'll support whatever decision you make with the child."

"Tay."

"No, Joa. If our kids are gonna be siblings then, I have to be ok with it." He turned me around to face him.

"I messed up and you taught me a lesson. I wish, you didn't have to because a nigga was fucked up but I got the message."

"I'll never be your first baby mother but.-" He placed his finger on my lips.

"You are my first baby mother."

"How?"

"Tay, you were the first woman to have my seed inside you. We may not have kept the baby but you were still the first. Yes, she may be having one physically but you'll always be my first." I understood what he was saying and I wish we kept the baby. Not that it would change what he did or maybe it would've. I guess we'll never know.

"I told you, your ass would be pregnant."

"You did." I smiled and stared at him.

"I didn't know until recently, which hurts me even more because I had no business being with someone else."

"Tay, you didn't know."

31

"I know but if I wasn't trying to hurt you, it never would've happened and I wouldn't be dealing with a maniac." He took the rag and started to wash me up.

"After you get dressed, you no longer live here."

"Huh?"

"Everything will be given to the Salvation army and any new clothes, shoes, purses or anything else you may need will be purchased brand new. Your truck has already been taken to the chop shop and you won't be at the club unless someone, mainly me or Menace is there with you. When you leave the house, there's a tracker on every vehicle and I'm ordering you a pair of diamond studs that you'll keep in your ear. They too, will have a tracking device. The only man in your life is me and my son you're carrying. Any questions?" He rinsed the water off, grabbed a towel, wrapped it around me and carried me in the room.

"Ummm, I don't think so. Joa, are you sure?"

"I've never been more sure about anything in my life." He began to dry me off.

"When Dynasty called to tell me she thought something happened to you, I felt like I couldn't breathe. Taylor, I don't care how long you hold a grudge for my mistake but what I do know, is we're still getting married." He got down on one knee and opened a little black box. I covered my mouth at the brand-new diamond ring. It was pear shaped and fucking humungous.

"This ain't Jamaica and I can't make love to you right now, but I wanna make sure you know I'm in this for life. Taylor Thomas, will you marry me?"

"Yes, Joakim Reeves. I'll be your wife." He slipped the ring on my finger.

"I love you so much baby." I kissed him all over his face and then placed a sloppy one on his mouth.

"Tay, if we didn't have somewhere to be, I swear, I'd fuck the shit outta you. I got you later." I smiled and glanced down at the ring.

"I have the other ring." He handed me my underclothes, a pair of leggings and a sweater to throw on.

"Toss that shit."

"Joa."

33

"Taylor, I would never propose with the same one or even expect you to keep it. You have a new ring for a reason."

"When did you get this one?"

"A few days after I got that one. I knew you'd still be my wife." He helped me slide my leg in the pants. They stretched at the bottom due to the cast but it was fine.

"How did you know I was here?"

"Ma, told me. Menace called, to tell her we couldn't find you and she told us you were here. After she cursed both of us out for not informing her sooner, they left."

"Left?"

"They knew I wasn't gonna let anything happen to you."

"Joakim, I went to tell him what we had was over and he flipped. He damaged some of the nerves in my hand and tossed me out the truck. He said if I tell you where he may or may not be, he'll catch me slippin and kill me. Joa, I'm scared."

"You have every right to be but I'm not about to let you outta my sight unless its with your brother."

34

"Do you know him?"

"Who? The guy that took you?" He put on his sweats.

"Yea."

"I have no idea. There are a few people named Donnell I know but we're not beefing. Why what's up?" I told him how he knew exactly who Joakim was and about the baby.

"What's his last name?"

"I can't even tell you."

"Really Tay?" I shrugged my shoulders.

"The only persons information I need to know, is yours and my brothers."

"You got that. Do you have a picture of him?"

"No but he did snap a photo of me at the restaurant. Do you know why he did that?"

"The only thing I can think of, is he's gonna figure out a way to send it to me and make it like you're cheating. Let's talk about this later." He pressed his lips on mine and carried me down the steps and out the door.

Once he placed me in the car, I noticed three huge moving trucks coming in the driveway. I looked at him go inside and return five minutes later. He kissed my cheek, put the key in the ignition and told me to say goodbye to my house and things. I asked where were my personal things, like my computer, important paperwork and things like that. He said, he had everything where we were going and not to worry. I smiled, laid my head on the seat and let my fiancé take me to my happily ever after.

Joakim

"Where are we?" Taylor asked when I parked in the driveway of the new house.

"This is our new house." She snapped her head.

"I thought you got rid of it or." I pulled her closer to me.

"If I got rid of it, then it meant I gave up on you and that was never an option." I slid my tongue in her mouth.

"Shit." My phone started to vibrate.

"Its ok. I wanna look inside." She opened the door.

"You're not gonna answer her?"

"Nope! I told her to contact me when she's in labor." I lifted her up and carried her all around the house. She was gonna take too long.

"Who's room is this?" I put her down.

"This is our baby's room. I left it for you to decorate."

"Really?"

"Yup. You have a lotta time but you can get started whenever."

"Come here." We walked in another room, which was the last room.

"Joa, this is nice." She referred to the master bedroom. I had it decorated in all her favorite colors. The rug even matched the bedroom set.

"I had to make sure it was nice enough for you to stay." She wrapped her arms around me.

"Anything you give me is nice and appreciated. Especially; this child and ring." I sat her on the bed.

"Taylor, the only reason I couldn't commit sooner is because I didn't wanna hurt you."

"What you mean?"

"I was still fucking different women and even though you never came second, I didn't wanna make you my girl, yet. Then, I messed up with Candy and hurt you anyway." She put her head down.

"I have issues with my pops leaving me at a young age and never looking back. I didn't want that with my kids. If I made a child with someone, she would be my wife and the only woman to bare my children. At least, my kids would grow up in a two-parent household. Tay." I made her look at me.

"It may be a dumb reason to you but its not to me. You deserved my full attention and I couldn't give it to you right away. Now that you've shown me, you can leave, I never want my heart broke again. I'll do any and everything to make sure you keep a smile on that pretty face. You and my children are my main concern and I love you even more, for sticking this shit out with me."

"Joa."

"No Tay. I'm sure its gonna be hard helping me raise another woman's child but please don't give up and leave."

"I won't. You are the only man I want and I'm partly to blame." I tried to speak but she cut me off.

"I didn't know about the abandonment issue but as far as, sleeping with other women, I attributed to it. I should've never been ok with it and shut shit down. I wanted you in my life so bad, I was willing to accept whatever you gave me. Was I weak for you? Hell yea and I still am. But I won't tolerate another woman saying she's carrying your child or you

39

sleeping around. If that's not outta your system, then let me go and if we find our way back, then so be it."

"Oh, its outta my system for sure. I don't want anyone but you and I hope you feel the same."

"I do." She lifted her shirt up and attempted to unsnap her bra.

"Not right now. I got you later."

"Joa, I want some right now." I laughed and stood her up. She put her shirt back on.

"You're gonna get it and when you do, no begging me to stop." She sucked her teeth. I carried her back down the steps and to the car. We still had a few stops to make and I couldn't wait to get home and give her exactly what she wanted.

****

"What the fuck you calling my phone for?" I pushed the door open at Candy's house. She tried to close it when I walked in and I stood right there to make sure she didn't.

"Joakim, I wanted some help putting the crib together." I'm still taking my kid so I don't know why she buying shit.

"You should've had them put it together."

"Why, when I have a man to do it?"

"Then why he ain't over here doing it?"

"You play too much. When are you going to upgrade me to a bigger spot and why haven't you brought the baby anything?" I looked at her to see if she were serious.

"I'm saying Joakim, if this were your precious Taylor, I'm sure she'd have it."

"You're absolutely right because she has her own money and if she didn't, she damn sure wouldn't depend on a man to get her shit. But since you wanna bring her up, I'd give that woman anything she asked for, without hesitation, you know why?" I stood in her face.

"Because she stuck with a nigga through everything. She kept her cool and hasn't beat your ass yet, like she wants to and she fucks the shit outta me. Something, you or no other woman could ever do." I could tell her feelings were hurt.

"You got some good pussy Candy and can make a nigga nut but that's all. Taylor, has a nigga ready to pass out

41

after sex and I can't lie, sometimes I do. Her shit is lethal and I'm not fucking that up for someone else to get it."

"Well, word on the street is another nigga already had it."

"Who told you that?" She picked her phone up and showed me some photo on her Facebook with Taylor at the restaurant. He wasn't in the photo but you saw a man's hand on the table. It had to be the day Taylor told me about. I knew it was coming but how did she get it? Taylor doesn't do social media and has some web designer do the one for her club.

"Where did you get this?" She became extremely nervous.

"It was on Facebook and someone tagged me."

"Tagged you for what though?"

"I don't know and who cares. The bitch fucking other niggas and you chastising me." Once she called her a bitch, I slammed her against the wall. Her robe fell open, exposing she was naked underneath. She had the nerve to smirk.

"Don't say shit about her again and you better not approach her with anymore of your bullshit." I let her go.

42

"Let me make you feel good daddy."

"Not! I'm good." She dropped to her knees and pulled down my sweats and boxers.

"Get the fuck up." She was only able to put the tip in her mouth before I backed away, pulled my sweats up and tightened the shit outta the string.

"She may be good but you're a man and that dick still gets hard for me."

"My dick will get hard seeing any bitch naked. It doesn't mean, I'm gonna fuck."

"You know you miss me." She ran and threw her hands around my waist. I knocked them away.

"This is my last time telling you. Don't hit my line again until you're in labor. If you do, I'll drag you to the fucking hospital myself and make them induce your stupid ass. Stop playing with me Candy. I'll fuck around and kill you sooner than later." I walked to the door.

"Joakim, are you really done with me?"

"Yes I am. Now, try me with this bullshit again." I slammed the door and went to my car. That was a close call. I won't dare disrespect Taylor again. I pulled off thinking of

how I'm gonna tell her what went down. Regardless; if she did

or not, I have to tell her because I can see Candy being spiteful.

Menace

"You good?" I asked Dynasty when she came down the steps this morning. She had been staying with me since leaving the hospital a few days ago.

"Yea. What you doing today?"

"I have to make a few stops around my businesses, go to the warehouse, and link up with Joakim. Why, what's up?" She shrugged her shoulders.

"You gonna miss me?"

"Maybe but I'm gonna miss this more." She stood, slid her shorts down, pull my dick out and grinded her bottom half. It didn't take long for me to wake up. Dynasty had that type of pussy to wake me up outta a dead sleep, because its so damn good.

"He's gonna miss you too." I squeezed her ass cheeks and helped her slide down.

"Mmmm." We both moaned out.

"Are you ever gonna tell me you're pregnant?" She stopped riding and looked at me.

"How did you know? My mom told you right?" I smiled because I was guessing. Her pussy was always gushy and good but its definitely a different feeling when a baby's inside.

"Don't stop ma." I guided her hips.

"I was but you were still looking for Taylor. Ahhh fuck." She yelled out when I pushed deeper.

"Take this dick." I smacked her backside and lifted her up and slammed her down on it.

"Menace, you feel so good. Sssssss." She bit down on her lip and I had to change positions because my ass was about to cum. The first time we had sex in the club is the only time, I came that fast and I don't wanna have it happen again. My ego, can't take it.

"Bend over, lift your right leg on the couch and turn around to look at me." She did what I said.

"Damn, you're so fucking sexy to me. And now my baby is inside you. Shit, you're stuck ma." I pulled out slow and went in hard. She loved that shit too. Her juices came gushing out.

46

"I love you Menace." She grabbed the couch and held on for dear life as I went harder and faster. I wanted to yank her head back but she still had he stitches in and I had to be careful not to bust them. We had no business fucking as it is but oh well.

"Say it again." I whispered in her ear.

"I love you. Shittttt."

"I love you too." I pulled out, laid her on the plush rug and took full advantage of her body. I ended up staying in the house with her all day. I'm not sure if us saying those three words made us wanna stay up under one another or not. But I wasn't complaining. I stared down at her sleeping and smiled. Her and my sister would be pregnant together. This is gonna be some funny shit.

****

"About time you brought your ass out the house. Got that chick laid up and now you barely come out." Joakim joked.

"What the fuck ever. You haven't been out either."

"Shit, I had to make up with Taylor. Even with her hurt ankle and messed up hand, she still does me good."

"Yo, get the hell outta here with that shit."

"I'm just saying, she got that ring, house, baby and bank account for a reason." I waved him off and opened the office door.

"Did you tell her yet?" He fell on the loveseat.

"I don't know how. She's gonna flip the fuck out and assume I wanted it."

"Again, you don't give her enough credit. You better tell her before Candy does because it won't sound good coming from her."

"I know." He called me the other day and told me the shit Candy did when he went over there. It seemed innocent to me and he stopped her but I can hear Taylor saying it never should've happened. In my opinion, its only right for him to let her know and get it over with. For some reason, when the chick tells the woman, it sounds so much worse. I don't know if it's because they taunt the woman or feel like they still have the dude. Whatever the case, it's not good to hold it in.

For the rest of the day, he and I went over shipments and other business ventures. I made plans to give my sister a salon but he took over and was looking for a spot. Today, I was meeting with a realtor to see some more empty spaces for Dynasty. She enjoyed modeling for the lady and wanted to open a photography studio. She had the money due to the lawsuit, yet; I wanted to buy it for her and let her save her money.

The thing, I loved about Dynasty is she was a go getter. She came home from jail and got on her grind right away. She never expected anything from anyone and that was something to admire from the start. I caught her a few times looking online and different spaces to rent and camera equipment. I had no problem sharing my money with her because she's worth it, in my eyes. It may seem fast to others but God put her in my path for a reason. I don't know if its to build with her or not. Whatever the case, I appreciated the hell outta him for it.

"Do you think its big enough?" Joakim asked, going in and outta rooms looking. The realtor was staring at him and smiling. He wasn't paying her any mind.

"I think it is. Shit, there's an upstairs with a few extra rooms, and at least five different rooms down here, with a reception area and conference room. If she wants a bigger spot later, I'll get her one. This should be good enough to start. How much is the price to own this property?"

"Wait! If he buys this, he can make it bigger, right?"

"Yes. He can do whatever he wants."

"We'll take it."

"Nigga, she didn't even give a price."

"It doesn't matter. This lot is huge." He pointed outside.

"I can add Taylor's salon next door and if they want something else on the remainder part, we can do that."

"That's an excellent idea. You do know, with the redevelopment they're doing, a lot of people will be here and come into their businesses."

"More people, means more money." Both of us stared out the window.

"That means, I'm gonna have to get this knocked down and rebuilt." Joakim looked at me.

"You think, I'ma let your girl have a brand-new building and mine won't? Not only is it not fair, I probably won't hear the end of it."

"You're right. What about putting a small coffee shop in the middle? Women love coffee and that other girly shit."

"Who gonna run it?"

"We can find someone to do it." He had all the damn answers.

"You know, Valley's girl works at the diner. I bet she can take a few online classes for business and have the shit running with no problem." I told him and he agreed. Shit, I was gonna have Dynasty do the same thing. At least, they'll be able to learn the business part. I told the lady we'd take it and signed on the dotted line. I couldn't wait to surprise her with it but I'm gonna wait until its finished.

****

"Menace, when are you bringing Dynasty by?" My mother asked soon as I opened the door to Taylor and Joakim's new place.

"I don't know. Shit, you ain't make no food." She smacked me on the back of the head.

"Menace, where's Dy?" Taylor came out the kitchen.

"Home. Damn, y'all not happy to see me?"

"Boy, we see you all the time. Now, that both of them are pregnant, I'm excited. We need to shop for baby furniture, clothes and anything else they need."

"Ma, Joakim and I already started looking."

"Dynasty, has been looking at things too."

"What the fuck y'all talking about? I'm shopping for my house. I'm not going to be forced to watch my grand babies over here all the time." Taylor and I, both busted out laughing.

"Shit. Both of you got me fucked up." She continued talking shit as she walked in the kitchen.

"Where's yo man?"

"Where you think?" She pointed to the basement.

"Menace?"

"Yea."

"Is he ok?"

"As far as, I know. What's up?"

"Ever since he came and got me, he's been distant and I don't know why? Do you think he's not ready? Maybe, we should've waited to move in together."

"He has a lot going on with the Candy shit. I don't think it has anything to do with you." She had glassy eyes.

"Taylor, you know he worships the ground you walk on. Don't look for shit that's not there." She nodded. I hugged her and went down stairs. He was lifting weights with the music blasting. The good thing about his basement is, it was soundproof. I walked over and shut the music off. He turned around and gave me a head nod.

"You didn't tell her, did you?" He slammed the weight down.

"Nah."

"Bro, you have to tell her."

"Man, every time I get home she's either got dinner cooking, or standing in the doorway waiting for me in something, that's hard to refuse."

"You need to do it soon. She thinks you may feel like, y'all are going too fast or some shit. She said you're distant."

"Fuck!"

"Nigga, you didn't cheat so why is it so hard for you to do it?"

53

"I can't even tell you."

"Don't tell me you fucked around and did."

"What? Hell no. I can't even tell you why I'm nervous about telling her when nothing happened. That shit is gonna hurt her and I don't want her to lose the baby." I ran my hand over my head. I understood but I see the shit turning out bad if he doesn't tell her. Oh well, I tried to talk to him about doing it and if he doesn't want to, I sure as hell can't make him. I'll sit back and let this shit play out. And trust me when I say, its not gonna play out the way he wants it to.

Quana

"Ok. So you're telling me that he has someone to do, drop offs on Wednesday and Friday?" I asked my cousin Block. We were dead set on getting Menace. At first, I thought about going to the cops but then I'd lose out on getting the money.

"Yes. During those days, the people at the secret warehouse.-"

"Hold up. There's a secret warehouse?"

"Listen Quana, Damn!"

"Ok. Go ahead."

"At the secret warehouse, is where the people who bag, weigh and cook the stuff. Once they're done, some of the product goes in another room where it's bagged into the little ass dime and nickel bags. The rest, goes in a different room where its made into a block. They sell those by the weight. After all that, they pack the stuff in boxes like they're grocery items. You know put boxes of cereal on top and things like that. Last but not least; on Sundays, different U-Haul trucks come,

55

pick the stuff up and distributes them to different trap houses and even to businesses."

"Businesses?"

"Yup. Menace ain't no fucking drug dealer Quana. He is a got damn kingpin. When I say he's the man, HE IS THE FUCKING MAN." I knew he was a Kingpin but damn. The shit my cousin is telling me sounds crazy.

"Wow! How did I not know all this in the five years we were together?"

"It's because you were too busy shopping and looking down on others. Instead, what you should've been doing is paying attention and accompanying him on more than vacations."

"But…"

"But nothing. You can't cry over spilled milk now. All you can do is help me find a way to intercept at least one of those trucks. That way we'll be able to find someone to buy it at a reasonable price."

"Ok you're bugging."

"How is that?" He took a pull of the blunt he smoked.

"I thought we would go to the house and take money from the safe or some shit like that. You tryna pull off some dead presidents' shit. Moving trucks and shit. Who the hell gonna by it? If he's a kingpin like that, won't someone know whose product it is?"

"Man, niggas don't care. Especially; if I sell it by the weight and at a lower price. They'll jump right on it. Have some faith girl." He continued smoking like he had this shit planned out perfectly. It sounded good but executing the plan itself, is a whole other ballgame.

"Fine! Where is this other warehouse?"

"That's the only problem." I gave him the side eye.

"I've only been there once."

"ONCE!" Nigga you got me souped up and ready to go to war over this and you don't even know where it's at. You sound crazy."

"Quana, I got this. Relax." I waved him off and stepped back in the house. My mom had her arms folded and was staring like she knew what we were planning.

"I don't wanna know what you two idiots are thinking about doing and I don't care. Just make sure my grandson isn't affected." She walked away and left me standing there.

"Aunty Quana, can we go for a ride?" I looked down at my nephew and smiled. That bitch may have taken my brother but at least a real woman, left an heir behind. I grabbed his hand, my purse and headed out.

****

"You are getting big. Are you excited yet?" I asked Candy. She asked me to stop by because of course her ass had some tea.

"Yes and no." She closed the door.

"No, I'm not happy because he won't upgrade me. He won't answer when I call and I don't have anyone to put this furniture together." I looked down on the floor at the baby stuff in her extra bedroom.

"Ok so what's the yes for?" The devious smile on her face only made me place one on mine.

58

"So he came over the other day to tell me not to call him unless I'm in labor. And to tell me not to say shit to Taylor."

"The precious girlfriend." I was being sarcastic.

"Exactly. Anyway, he tossed me against the wall, my robe opened, his dick grew and.-"

"And what bitch? Don't keep me hanging." I was in suspense.

"And he had on sweats, I pulled them and his boxers down and slid his dick in my mouth."

"Whattttttttt? Get the fuck outta here. How long did he let you suck it? Oh, this is good. Did you fuck? Details bitch. Details."

"I was only able to get the tip in and he pulled away." I tried to grab it, to keep him there but he was too fast."

"Oh, that's nothing. I thought you had something." She smirked.

"Technology let's you do a lot of things." She passed me her phone and you saw him toss her against the wall, her robe opened, she pulled his clothes down, got in a squatting

59

position and you can see her put it in. The video showed everything she said except him stopping her. If she didn't tell me, I would assume she kept going.

"You my bitch. When you sending this?"

"I'm not."

"Ugh, why?"

"Because I'm gonna wait for Just the right time."

"And when is that?"

"Who knows? Maybe my baby shower."

"But he may not come."

"He may not but his mom will. The heffa can't stand me but she told me I better invite her or she'll make sure I get my ass whooped."

"Well, invite her. Who knows? Maybe he'll come with the bitch."

"And if not, guess who's getting the video?"

"That's what I'm talking about."

"Hey, I have a doctor's appointment in an hour. You wanna go?"

"I guess. It's not like I have anything else to do."

"Gee thanks."

"Girl bye. Stop being dramatic and get ready."

I turned the TV on and waited for her to get dressed. It wasn't much on, which left me sitting there to think about everything going on. My brother's murderer is free and with my man. My cousin wants us to go on a suicide mission and my mother doesn't care what happens to me, as long as, my nephew isn't affected. I get it but damn does anyone care what I'm going through?

Candy came out and we went to the doctors. Joakim showed up and you could tell he had disgust and hate for her. I don't know why, when he had been sleeping with her for a long time. I would've thought he felt something but maybe not. The doctor told them they were having a girl and she was ecstatic while he had no expression.

"Joakim, are we gonna name her together?" He sucked his teeth and opened the door to leave.

"Don't be like that boo. I promise not to tell Taylor what we did." He chuckled.

"One and a half more months is all I'm gonna say." He winked and slammed the door. He didn't deny anything but then again, it doesn't mean shit.

"What does that mean?" I asked and she looked spooked.

"Let's go." She wiped the gel off, pulled her jeans up and tried to smile. The way he said it was normal but I'm meant something different to her. Oh well, that's her shit. Let me get her home before he kills both of us.

Candy

Before everyone starts judging, let me tell you my story. Joakim and I met two years ago at Taylor's club and he told me there was no one else. After the first two times on the phone, we slept together and yes it was the bomb. I mean shit, any man who can make you cum in one night as much as he can, is a keeper for sure.

Anyway, after about nine months of us sexing each other and going on vacations, I wondered why he wouldn't claim me as the girlfriend. He told me we were only fucking and not to ask again. Low and behold, a few months later him and Taylor began to show signs of them being together. He would answer her whenever we were out. If she needed something he'd drop whatever he was doing and run to her. On plenty of occasions, he wouldn't see me for days and when I asked why, he told me none of my business.

I only found out about them because Quana told me she saw them at Menace house making googly eyes at each other. Or she'd catch him talking really close and she would smile.

63

What took the cake is me bothering her at work about it and he'd defend her every time. It didn't matter if she cursed me out or not, it was always my fault.

That's why I made sure to pop holes in the condom when we were away. He thought he fucked me raw but drunk or not, he definitely strapped up. I was able to do it because he asked me to take them out his jeans and put it on. He fucked up because a bitch damn sure did my thing. Of course, I slept with a couple other guys but I made sure they strapped up. I only told them this was their baby because of the money I received. They were the dumb ones for believing me.

I loved messing with Taylor about my pregnancy too. The only thing is, she's still winning. He won't leave her alone and I'm the one who's missing out on having a baby daddy in my kids life. I know she's the one telling him to stay away from me because we have or had great sex, so I know that's not the reason he stopped coming around. Whatever hold she has on him bothers the hell outta me. I did invite both of them to my baby shower though. I had a treat and I couldn't wait to show it.

****

"You ready for the show?" Quana asked as she helped me get ready for my baby shower. I was having it at a community center since my apartment didn't have a backyard and I didn't want that many people in here.

"Of course. The question is, are you?" I asked because Joakim said he was coming with Taylor and Menace would be there too. I assumed he'd bring Dynasty and I think Quana was hoping he would as well. She wanted to expose her of being the one who murdered her brother. I told her he probably knew already but she said, she wanted to be sure. In her mind, he'd feel bad and dump the chick.

"You know it." She went in my bathroom to shower and get dressed since she spent last night here. After she finished it was my turn and shortly after, we'd be on our way.

We arrived at the place around one thirty even though it started at one. I'm supposed to be late and I'm glad I was because all eyes were on me. It wasn't packed but it was quite a bit of folk from my job, my mom, her friends, a few relatives, Joakim and his people. I glanced over at Taylor, and her,

Dynasty and some other chick were sitting at a table talking. I rolled my eyes and walked over to my baby daddy who was engaged in a conversation with Menace and some other guys.

"Hey boo." He ignored me.

"Joakim." I whined.

"What Candy? What do you want?"

"I want you to sit by me when I open gifts."

"Fine now beat it!" I stared at Quana who was smirking.

"Hello ladies." I spoke to Taylor individually.

"I'm glad you could make it." She gave me a fake smile.

"Did Joakim tell you about us?"

"Back the hell up Candy." I heard Joakim bark behind me.

"What did you two do Candy?" I saw the blood drain from his face.

"I'll tell you later. Let's open our gifts boo." I made my way to the mama to be chair and took a seat.

"What are you tryna prove Candy?" He whispered in my ear.

"Nothing Joakim. I don't think you should be keeping secrets from her. That is unless you plan on allowing me to feel you inside me again." I smirked and saw the look of hate on his face.

"So which one should we open first?" I saw him walk away and waited for Quana to come over. I told her what happened and we both got a kick outta it.

After opening all the gifts, playing a few games and blowing kisses to my baby daddy, I thought it was time to show my ass one last time. I waited for everyone to have a seat and watched Quana put iPads on each table. Mind you there were only ten tables and I only had five. I had the people who didn't have one stand at the other tables to see. Of course, Taylor and her crew had one.

"Ok everyone. As you all know, my grandmother couldn't be here so she sent a message VIA email. It's supposed to have the gift on the email she sent me."

"A gift on an email don't even sound right." I heard the bitch with Taylor yell. I sucked my teeth and had everyone go to the internet browser and type in my email address. I could

67

see Dynasty doing it because Taylor had her arms folded, staring at me.

"Now open the link that says *To Candy*." I saw people fingers moving and waited. Joakim stared at me and I gave him the finger.

"Let me make you feel good daddy." I heard. I was happy, Quana made sure all the volumes were turned up.

"Oh my God! I think you gave us the wrong link." I walked over to the lady who said it.

"Oh my. I guess it was the wrong link. We'll have to get that fixed. Ok everyone. Let's move on. What's next Quana?" I turned and Taylor punched me so hard in the face I fell into someone.

"You went through a lot to make this happen huh?" I stood up and caught some of the blood dropping from my nose.

"Well guess what? Since you two can't seem to stay away from each other or keep your hands off, you may as well be together." She walked over to Joakim.

"I thought it was me."

"Tay."

"No Joa. I thought maybe you didn't wanna move me in so fast or I did something wrong. Maybe from being with the other dude, I don't know. But you were standoffish and I couldn't figure out why. Now I see. Goodbye and I mean it this time." She took something off her hand and placed it in his. Did he ask her to marry him? When she walked off my heart literally stopped beating when he took off in my direction. His hands were around my throat so fast, I couldn't run even if I tried.

"Joakim let her go." I heard his mom yell. His grip became tighter and his face was full of evil.

"Joakim now." He pressed and it felt like I was dying. My eyes seemed like they were gonna pop out.

"Alright, I think she gets it." Menace finally came over and removed his hands and I fell to the ground.

"I'm gonna kill you the second that baby comes out your fucking stomach." He kicked me in the head and that was it.

****

"Are you crazy?" I heard some woman say as she stood over me. Why was I still here? Why hadn't no one taken me to the hospital?

"Excuse me!" I rolled on my knees and stood up.

"Why would you do that? And then you show his woman and everyone in here. You have no idea what he's gonna do to you?"

"Who are you?"

"It doesn't matter. I only came over here to tell you this." She was standing in my face and that's when I realized who she was. It was the bitch who sat at the table with Taylor.

"Taylor is the only woman he wants and everyone knows it but you. What you pulled is only making him hate you more. How do you think this child will feel growing up without its mother?" She smirked and walked off. The bitch had the nerve to turn around and mouthed the words, *you're dead.*

"Candy" I heard my mother's voice.

"Yea."

WHAP! WHAP! I held my face.

"What the fuck is wrong with you?

"Ma!"

"What you did was childish and I need you to tell me right now, what you got out of it!" I sucked my teeth.

"Is he gonna come back to you? What about him raising the kid with you? What can you possibly think you'd gain by doing that? And you did it in front of people you work with, older folk and most of all his woman."

"FUCK HER!"

"Why Candy? Huh? Why?"

"He's supposed to be my man. She stole him." My mom busted out laughing.

"Even I know that's not true. That man worships the ground she walks on." I looked at her.

"Oh people talk. Anyway, you destroyed their relationship because your miserable. I hope your daughter doesn't grow up and acquire these stalking and ho like tendencies." She walked off and left me standing there. Did I go too far? Would Joakim kill me? I do know, my ass needs to hide after I deliver but who will help me? A man came to mind

and I'm sure he'll have no issues accommodating me.

Dynasty

"I knew that bitch had something up her sleeve." Taylor said pacing back and forth in the parking lot. We were waiting on Jen to come out.

"What are you gonna do?"

"I don't know. I felt something wasn't right with Joa but I wasn't sure. And with us getting back on track, I didn't wanna accuse or badger him about anything. Do you think he did it because I slept with Donnell?"

"I don't think its what it seems." She stopped pacing and looked at me.

"I know what the video depicted but did you notice how it stopped abruptly? Something else went down and it could've been him stopping her." She gave me a crazy look.

"Think about it. We all know how hard he's fought to keep you in his life. I don't see him messing it up, especially; for someone like her. I mean Taylor, he brought your spoiled ass a house, a new truck, a brand-new ring, which you said is bigger than the other one and he's been up under you to make sure there were no insecurities on your part."

"Didn't Joakim tell you he was going over there that day?" Jen asked coming out the door.

"Yea but."

"Yea but what? Do you really think he'd risk doing anything with her, knowing she'll tell you the first chance she got? He loves you Taylor." She started crying.

"I know he does but this shit is hard. How can I tell him not to see if she's ok, when that is his child, she's carrying?"

"You don't. Take your ass over there with him. I would." Jen had her arms folded like she was the one affected.

"Then it'll seem like I don't trust him."

"It's not him you don't trust. It's her and as you can see, you shouldn't." I told her and we all got in the car. She rode over with him but refused to go home.

"Anyway, when you left, he tried to kill her."

"WHAT?" We both shouted. I ran out with her so I didn't even see it.

"Yup. Look."

74

"Jen, I know damn well you didn't record it."

"The hell, I didn't." We all started laughing.

"As soon as, Taylor handed him the ring, my ass knew he was about to do something so I hit record. That's what her ass gets. Fuck that bitch." Jen handed Taylor the phone because she was driving.

"Pull over Jen." Taylor hollered and she stopped on the side so we look.

The video showed Joakim choking the life outta Candy and once Menace pulled him away, he promised to kill her and then kicked her in the head. I shook my head because Candy had really pissed him off. I couldn't believe my eyes and I made a mental note to never piss him off. Shit, if he gets that angry over Taylor, I wonder if Menace is the same.

Jen was about to pull off when someone hit the back of the car. Now me being the ex-convict was nervous because I didn't need no bullshit and once we saw her get out the car, all of us knew what it was. I sent my man a text and told him to get to where we were fast or I'm going to jail.

"What the fuck is wrong with you?" Jen had hopped

out the car, with both of us behind her. I could hear my phone

ringing but ignored it because what I was about to do, required

me not to.

"You were in the way."

"In the way. Bitch we're on the shoulder and.-"

"Jen, she didn't mean you were in the way literally, as

far as, the car." I walked closer to her.

"This has everything to do with me being in the way.

Ain't that right Quana? I'm in the way between you and

Menace?"

"As a matter of fact, you.-" She couldn't finished her

sentence because I popped her in the face and kept hitting. She

tried to get a hit in but it was no way she could. I grabbed her

head, like she did mine and banged it into the side of the car

door.

"Beat that ass Dynasty." I heard Jen yelling out.

"Got dammit." I heard and felt him pull me off. I gave

the bitch one hard kick in the stomach and spit in her face.

"Y'all really let her fight with my baby in her stomach?" Menace yelled at both of them.

"Fuck that Menace. She hit the back of Jen's car and started talking shit to her. You know it was bound to happen." Taylor tried to cop a plea but he wasn't tryna hear it.

"Are you ok? Did she hit you in the stomach?" He was checking me over.

"No, I'm ok."

"Get in the truck."

"Menace, I'm sorry."

"Get... In... The... Fucking... Truck..." He gave me a look and I walked right to Jen's car. At first, I was going to grab my things but changed my mind. Who the hell was he talking to like that? I made my way down the street. Don't ask me where I was going, knowing he lived in the middle of nowhere and my house is a half hour away.

"DYNASTY!" Jen and Taylor were both yelling my name. All of a sudden, I heard a screech behind me and a door close. I turned around and was yanked up by my shirt.

"I won't ever put my hands on you Dynasty but I swear to God if you don't get in the fucking truck, its gonna be a problem."

"I don't.-"

"I don't give a fuck what you want. Either walk or I'm putting you in it." I stood there with my arms folded. He lifted me up, put me in the back seat and I watched him throw the child lock on it. A car pulled up on the side of him and it was Jen and Taylor. I tried to roll the window down and it was locked too. He said a few words to them and got in.

"I wanna go home."

"You will. Trust me." He said it in a way I didn't care for. He drove for a little while and pulled up at the hospital.

"Why are we here?"

"Because of the dumb shit you did. I have to make sure my kid is ok." He opened the back door and helped me out.

"Look at this shit." He pointed to my shirt that had a rip in it and the scratch on my face. We went inside and they sent me upstairs. The doctor hooked me up and both of us were smiling as she did an ultrasound. I found out about the pregnancy and my first appointment was next week.

I had to stay there for a couple of hours because Menace told her about the fight and she laid into me about not allowing it to happen again. All the bad things that could happen the next time. I could tell he was mad and he had every right to be but she deserved that ass whooping. Maybe, I should've waited but the opportunity presented itself and I had to take it. Its not right and my child should've been the only thing on my mind, however; I only saw red when she got out the car.

"Remember what I said, Ms. Sutton." The doctor handed me the discharge papers and Menace waited for me to get dressed.

"I'm hungry."

"Didn't you eat at the baby shower?"

"I'm hungry again."

"What you want?"

"I have a taste for Subway."

"Lets go." He walked ahead of me and kept his face in the phone at the same time. Who the hell was texting him? I didn't even waste my breath but something told me it was his ex.

"Where are we going?" I asked after he left Subway and hopped on the highway.

"You're going home. That's what you wanted right?"

"Yea but I live with you." He chuckled like it was funny.

"Nah. I don't need a woman staying with me who don't care about her own well-being or my child's."

"Menace, I'm sorry but.-"

"There's no buts Dynasty. I know you wanted to get her back for what she did. Let me ask you this." He drove without looking at me.

"Did she put her hands on you?"

"No."

"Did she appear to jump at or provoke you to hit her?" I put my head down.

"Exactly! You couldn't wait until after you had the baby?"

"I wasn't thinking."

"No, you weren't. All you had on your mind was fighting her to make sure everyone knew you could fight. You couldn't let anyone think Quana beat you up, right? I mean, what else could it be?" I didn't respond because he was right. I did want everyone to know I could fight. I should've waited and did it later.

"Dynasty, if this is the type of woman you are, I can't be around." He put the truck in park at the house and looked at me.

"What?" I was pissed.

"I can't have this type of drama around and I won't."

"You mean to tell me, she didn't have any."

"That's just it Dy. She had a lot and I don't wanna deal with that shit again. You were everything I wanted in a woman. No drama and wanted to make your life better. Now you out here doing chicken head shit and I got too much going on, to worry about you fighting."

"So what you saying Menace because the way you're talking, it seems like you want us to be over." He ran his hand over his head.

"We need to take a break Dy." I felt the tears rolling down my face.

"Ummm, ok." He made me look at him.

"This isn't what I wanted and you know it."

"I can't tell."

"Dynasty, I moved you into my house. Gave you the code to my shit and came home to you and only you, every night. There's no woman out here I want but maybe you were right about moving too fast. You missed a lotta time out here and need to get your head right."

"Menace, I have my head on right and if you wanna be with someone else, just say it."

"This is what I'm talking about. I just told you, I don't want anyone else and you're making assumptions." His phone went off and I saw Quana's name pop up.

"I'm making assumptions huh?"

"Dy."

"Don't worry about it. Y'all were together for a long time and you were checking on her right?"

"Yes and no."

"Either you were or not? Were you checking on her?"

"Yea. You fucked her up pretty bad and.-"

"And who the fuck cares. She did the same shit to me and its only fair she received the same treatment. But to see you're checking on her makes me see shit for what it is."

"Dynasty, its not what you think."

"It no longer matters what I think because you made it clear as day, that she's still someone you care about." I grabbed my things and opened the door.

"I thought me fighting is what bothered you the most and I'm sure the baby is why." He tried to speak and I put my hand up.

"You still love her and I'll be damned if I compete with a woman who has spent five years with you. Regardless, if you love me or not, there's no competition." I closed the door and heard his open as I made my way to the door. He grabbed my arm.

"I don't want her."

"Go home, look yourself in the mirror and keep telling yourself that until you believe it."

"Dynasty."

"I was wrong for fighting her. I was. I also know, if you're not fucking with someone, you shouldn't care if she's ok or not. I didn't kill her so why bother? You know what Menace." I opened the house door.

"This is my own fault." I wiped my eyes.

"What was I thinking getting in a relationship fresh outta jail. I was so used to being alone, that I jumped right into one with a man who was fresh outta his own. You gave me the attention I missed. The lovemaking took over my brain and I couldn't fathom you being with another woman so I made sure to try and lock you down. I guess it didn't matter because look where we are now." I saw the sad look in his eyes for me.

"I'm in love with you Dynasty and she means nothing." I shook my head.

"No, you're not. You love being with a woman no one else can say they had. A woman, who was stupid enough to let you get pregnant. A woman, who will have to deal with you for the rest of her life because of this child. And a woman who desperately wanted a man and didn't care how fast she jumped in a relationship."

"Don't put words in my mouth."

"Deny it all you want and if that's what I see, you can't take that away from me."

"Fuck it. If this is what you want."

"What I want? You did this Menace."

"I said we needed to take a break but you're making this shit forever and that's not what I wanted. I needed you to get the bullshit out your system. You went overboard with me wanting her and all this other shit."

"I went overboard says the man, checking for his so-called ex. Would you be ok with me checking on Block after he put his hands on me?" His face cringed.

"Exactly. Do me a favor Menace?" He looked at me.

"From now on. Put yourself in my shoes when you're about to do dumb shit and figure out, how you'd feel if it were you."

"I'm done with this conversation Dy because you're.-"

"I'm what? Showing you what you don't wanna see."

"There's nothing to see." I shook my head.

"Goodbye Menace."

"The fuck you want from me Dynasty?" He was really mad. I don't know why when he's the one who made the decision to end us and when I'm ok with it, he's not.

"Nothing. Nothing at all." I closed the door and fell against it crying. I was so in love with him and whether he saw it or not; him checking on his ex is dead wrong. I'll admit to everyone how wrong it was to fight but I won't be blind to a man who still has feelings for his ex.

Five years is a long time and they won't go away quickly but responding and checking on her like she's still his woman, doesn't sit right with me and I won't allow him to do me dirty. People can say I'm overreacting and I don't care. I'm backing away before my hearts get broken, more than it already is.

"You ok?" I heard my mom ask.

"No." She sat next to me by the door and I laid my head on her shoulder explaining what happened.

"I agree with you Dynasty about him possibly still having feelings for her but it doesn't mean he wants her."

"So, I should be ok with him making sure she's ok?"

"That's a tough question. What if Jamal were alive and you were with someone else and he hears about something happening to you. Do you really think he wouldn't find out if you're ok?" I gave her the side eye.

"Ok, wrong analogy. Pretend it was someone else but you get where I'm going with it."

"What about him saying he needed a break."

"He said a break Dy and not let's be over forever. It seems like he wanted to make you sit and think about what you did. He knows you did time and doesn't wanna see you end up in jail again. Honey look." She lifted my head off her shoulder.

"Everyone isn't Jamal and he really does have your best interest at heart, whether you see it or not. The part with his ex, is a sticky situation and you have every right to feel the way you do. The question now is, what are you gonna do?"

87

"What you mean?"

"Are you gonna fight for him or let another woman stake claims?"

"Right now ma, I don't even care. Yes, I'm upset but he's right. I need to focus on myself and if I focus on that, I won't do anything." I stood up and made my way to the steps.

"Well, I'm here if you need to talk." I smiled and went to kitchen instead. I was still hungry and because I was so mad, I left the damn sandwich he got me in the truck. Oh well, I'm about to tear some leftover dinner up my mom left in the fridge. I'll probably get big as a house and I gave zero fucks.

Menace

I hopped in my truck and grabbed the phone. Quana was ringing my shot off the hook and I understood, wholeheartedly why Dynasty was upset. Here she whooped my ex's ass and I'm checking on her. Dynasty really fucked her up though. Her lip was busted, her nose looked like it was broke and she definitely had a gash on her forehead. Blood was leaking from different places on her face and I almost laughed.

Its not like I wanted to because she did deserve it but I also didn't need Quana going to the cops like she planned on doing, if I didn't come see her. Bad enough she was in the emergency room at the same hospital. If Dy knew that, she probably would've gone down there and fought her again. I've told Quana a few times she's gonna meet her match and no woman I dealt with, is gonna deal with her bullshit and now look. She's calling me to stop by and my dumb ass is in front of her mother's house. I was about to step out and she came out the door. Her nose was swollen, she had two black eyes and a bandage on her forehead. She had a slight limp and I cracked a smile before she came to the truck.

"What?" I rolled my window down.

"I can't sit inside." I blew my breath and unlocked the door. Something told me this wasn't a good idea but I went against my better judgement. She closed the door, folded her arms across her chest and sat there. After about ten minutes, I told her to get out if she wasn't gonna speak.

"How could you get her pregnant?" I looked at her.

"Are you serious right now?"

"Hell yea. I've been with you for five years and you barely fucked me without a condom and when you did, you made sure to pull out. This bitch.-"

"Watch it." Regardless of what Dynasty and I are going through, she'll never disrespect her in my presence. I started rolling a blunt because I damn sure needed one.

"And you're defending her?"

"I wouldn't allow anyone to disrespect you either when we were together, so go head with that shit." She sucked her teeth.

90

"A baby though Menace?"

"Quana, you only wanted a kid with me in hopes of keeping me around. Not once, during our relationship did you pressure me about a kid. Now you hear about this woman giving me one and you're in your feelings. Not only that, you purposely ran into the back of Jen's car to fuck with her." She waved her hand at me and I caught it.

"You are my past now Quana and this shit you're doing isn't ever gonna make me want you again. Its over and time for you to move on." I let her hand go.

"What if I don't want to?"

"I don't know what to tell you." I lit the blunt and took a pull.

"Why her Menace?"

"Why not?"

"She's the one who.-" I stopped her.

"I know exactly who she is and what happened in the past, so don't try and assassinate her character." She rolled her eyes.

"Did you know your brother was beating on her like that?" She turned to look at me.

"Did you?" I blew smoke out.

"She'd make him mad and my mom told her not to. We tried to get her away from but she stayed." I laughed at her stupidity.

"You believe a woman would stay with a man who constantly beat on her? What about Ruthie?"

"What about her?"

"Did you know about her too?"

"Menace, I couldn't control what Jamal did. Shit. She knew about his cheating ways and stayed."

"So, the nights she came to your moms' house to get away from him, wasn't a sign she tried to leave? Or her signing restraining orders, calling the cops and begging him to let her go, wasn't a sign?"

"None, of that was proven."

"Your brother had law enforcement on his side. He paid them to walk away." She didn't say anything.

"Do you know how she was able to be released?"

"Who cares?"

"You obviously did because you sent hella letters to the courthouse requesting she die in there." I could see the shocked look on her face.

"Her lawyer, was able to find all the loop holes, mistakes and fuck ups the police department and your brother did. I won't speak ill of the dead but your brother was foul as fuck and you know it." Her brother was known in the streets and on his way to being big time until his death. A lot of people hated him but he handled business very well.

"She didn't have to kill him." I saw her eyes watering. I knew she loved her brother but she was in denial about a lotta shit.

"It was her or him Quana."

"He should've killed her." I snapped my neck.

"What the fuck is wrong with you?"

"Then she wouldn't be giving you a baby and he'd be here." I had to take a minute to stare at her. What type of woman wishes death on someone for a dumb ass reason like that?

93

"Listen to yourself. If she didn't kill him, he would've killed her and then moved on to the next chick and did the same thing. You knew what he was doing and even about the kid. How do you think she felt as he abused her? And what do you think she felt hearing you mention another woman and child in that room, when you tried to get her to stay in jail? Then she sees the kid and he is a replica of your brother and birthed by her so called best friend?" She shrugged her shoulders.

"Ok, how do you think she felt when Block beat on her. Twice." She turned her head quickly.

"Oh, he didn't tell you that's why he got his ass beat?"

"No."

"I may have yoked you up a few times Quana and that's bad enough but I would never put my hands on you or any other woman like that." She sat in the passenger seat quiet. After I finished smoking I told her it was time to get out.

"Now what?"

"Now what, what? Stay away from Dynasty. She hasn't done anything to you. As far as, the beat down, you know damn well the time was coming for it." She had her phone in her hand. I grabbed mine that was ringing from Joakim.

"Do you still love me Menace?" I didn't answer and sent him a text, saying I'd hit him up in a few minutes.

"Yup." I said it without hesitation because I did.

"Then why can't we be together?"

"Because the way I love you is more in a friendly type of way. I don't wish bad on you, nor do I wanna be with you. Dynasty, is the only woman I want."

"But I love you and we can make it work. I promise to do everything you wanted."

"Even if I thought about trying again, my mind, heart and soul would be with another woman and it wouldn't be fair to you."

"Menace, please." She let the tears fall as she begged me to take her back and like usual, they did nothing for me. When Dynasty cried, all I wanted to do was hold her and say everything would be ok but she wasn't having it. I don't know what's different between the two because I was in love with Quana at one point but not once did her tears move me.

"Goodbye Quana and if you decide to press charges on her for this, I'll make sure to get the tape of you and Candy jumping her at Taylor's club. I'll also make you wish you were never born. Don't fuck with me."

"Really?"

"Really. I only came over here so you could see I wasn't playing games with you." I stepped out the truck, stretched and went over to her side to open the door. It didn't look like she wanted to get out and I'm not sitting out here any longer.

"Lets go. I got shit to do." I held her hand to step down. She wrapped her arms around my neck, stood on her tippy toes and kissed me. I pushed her back against the truck, slammed the door and went to the driver's side. This bitch was testing me. I rolled the window down before I pulled off.

"Oh, let your cousin know when I find him and Ruthie, I'm gonna kill both of them, slowly." Her mouth fell open as I pulled off. Ain't no way, either of them should be alive after the shit they did to Dynasty at the store. She said he was talking to her when Ruthie hit her but the way I see it is, they set the shit up to get her and I'm not letting it slide.

****

"When you going home to your man?" I asked Taylor who was lying on the couch, stuffing her face with chips and dip. She's been staying with my mom since the shit at Candy's baby shower and Joakim was bugging the fuck out.

"I am home."

"Your home is where your nigga at." She sat up.

"I don't have a nigga." She picked a chip up and chomped down on it.

"You may not have a nigga, but that nigga got you." She rolled her eyes.

"I told him to tell you Taylor."

"Then, why didn't he?"

"Look, he went there to tell her to stop calling him. He yoked her up and she dropped to get his clothes down. He was pulling them up and she put her mouth on it. He pulled away fast, cursed her out and left. The bitch must've edited the shit out." I could see her thinking about what I said.

97

"Anyway, he was scared you'd think he wanted it and leave him again. Girl you know that motherfucker don't want no one but your spoiled ass."

"I'm not spoiled." She threw the top to the dip at me.

"BULLSHIT! You have been all your life and I may have stopped entertaining it but he hasn't. He'll give you the damn sun if he could."

"Yea well, he doesn't know how to make good choices."

"Says the one who went out with the psychopath."

"MAAAAAA! Menace is down her making fun of what Donnell did to me." My mom came down the steps and popped me in the head.

"Boy, you know that shit is traumatic for her."

"Well, tell her to stop acting like a brat and go home to her man."

"I've been telling her to go home since the shower but you know she holds a grudge. If he wants her to come home, he'll have to come get her. I washed my hands with them two and their issues. What's going on with Dynasty and you?"

98

"Not a damn thing. I'm about to go meet her at the doctors."

"Do you speak?"

"Nope and I don't care."

"Yea right." Taylor said still chomping down on chips.

"Of course, I miss her but we both said some things to each other and maybe we do need time apart. Quana is a distraction and if Dynasty has it in her head that I want her, then nothing I say or do will change it. I'm not pacifying her thoughts. Its about my kid from here on out and nothing else."

"Ok then. What time is the appointment because I'm going." Taylor wiped her hands on the napkin and stood up.

"In an hour and who said you can come?"

"I did. Plus, I wanna see if she's having a girl or boy."

"You do know its too early right?"

"Miracles happen."

"Bye Taylor." I grabbed the remote on the couch and flipped through.

"You and Taylor are driving me crazy with your personal issues."

"Ma, I haven't even bothered you."

"No, but I've called to check on her and she's in love with you son." I sucked my teeth.

"She's scared and after she told me about you worrying about Quana, I'd feel the same."

"Nobody wants Quana ass."

"You may not want her but she wants you and just like Candy, she will not stop trying to destroy any relationship you end up in. Think about what you stopped fighting for and see if its worth it in the long run."

"What you mean?"

"Joakim has a kid on the way by a woman who he hates. The child will be back and forth from his house, to hers. I've known him all his life and he's always stated he didn't want his kids living in separate houses."

"I know."

"You used to feel the same." She kissed my cheek and walked away. I didn't want my child living separately but the way things are going, it may just happen.

I waited for Taylor and both of us drove to the doctor's office together. When we stepped out the truck, Dynasty was getting out with her mom looking sexy in her leggings and shirt. Her ass was fat and I wanted to smack it, just to watch it jiggle. Taylor punched me on the arm and told me to stop staring because it made her uncomfortable. Don't ask me how.

I made it to the door before them and held it open for everyone. Dynasty's mom smiled and mouthed the words, *she misses me* without her seeing. I told her the feelings were mutual.

Dynasty and Taylor sat next to one another and I watched how she smiled speaking of them being pregnant together. At least, I had no worries about her terminating it. She caught me staring a few times and would blush. It felt like we were just meeting and crushing on one another. The nurse called her to the back and all of us went. They took her vitals and had her change and lay on the table.

"Menace." I was talking on my phone with Joakim who said they heard someone tried to break in the warehouse.

"Yea." I went to wear she was.

101

"Can you undo the zipper on my shirt? Its stuck and I don't have a bra on, otherwise I would've asked my mom or Taylor to help."

"Turn around."

"Nigga don't fuck her in there." I laughed so hard the phone fell out my ear.

"What happened?"

"Nothing." I fixed the zipper and picked my phone up and told him, I'd call him back.

"Why aren't you wearing a bra?" I took the shirt and placed it on the chair. It wasn't see through and if she didn't mention it, I wouldn't have known.

"Because my chest is growing and they make my nipples itch. See." She uncovered her breasts and my mouth watered. I wanted her in the worse way and she knew, because the smirk told it all.

"You play too much." I passed her the gown.

"I'm serious Menace. Look." She started massaging them in a sexual manner and I peeked from behind the curtain

102

to see if her mom and Taylor was still there, and no one was in the room.

"You think this shit is funny?" I sat in the chair and pulled her on my lap.

"No. Sssssss." She moaned when my mouth latched on one of her titties.

"You miss this?" I placed my hand in between her legs and felt how wet she'd become.

"Yesssss. I'm getting ready to cum Menace."

"Hurry up." I whispered and placed her mouth on mine. She was driving me insane, fucking my fingers like it was my dick. She squeezed my neck and moaned in my mouth. Her face was now, in the crook of my neck.

"Stand up."

"I can't." I smiled and pulled the curtain back. There was still no one in the room. I carried her over to the table, grabbed some paper towels, wet them and wiped her down real quick. I took a seat next to her and asked her not to say anything else to me. Her voice was turning me on and after seeing how hard she came, I was ready to be all up in it.

103

"What's taking so long?" I went to open the door.

Taylor and her mom were standing there smirking.

"What?"

"About time. We had to send the doctor away twice."

Taylor pushed past me.

"Whatever."

"You got that nut huh?" Her mom was blunt with the shit and I could see how embarrassed Dynasty was.

After the appointment, we were all on our way out. I pulled her to the side and lifted her face. I didn't get to say two words to her, as the black SUV rode down the street and bullets were flying everywhere. I pushed her down and stayed on top of her until it stopped. I looked around and people were on the ground. I ran to check on my sister and she was ok but shaken up. I saw Dynasty running to her mom, who was about to stand up and saw the SUV coming back.

"DYNASTY GET DOWN!" She heard me and did what I said. I turned around and started shooting. I didn't have a lot of bullets but I damn sure struck someone because the truck ran into the telephone pole.

"Fuck!" I ran over to check on Dynasty and her mom. Taylor was under my truck so I knew she was good. I walked fast as hell, to the SUV and another car came flying down the road and my body felt the bullets tearing my flesh.

"MENACEEEEEEEE!" I heard Dynasty screaming as I hit the ground. You could hear the car screeching in the distance and sirens. I hope they make it in time.

Dynasty

"Dynasty, wait for the cops." I heard my mom yell but I couldn't. Once the car sped off that shot Menace, I had to make sure he was ok.

"Menace, baby. Are you ok?" I dropped down and he was on his side.

"MENACE!" I heard Taylor screaming and saw her running over.

"Why y'all screaming? I'm fine." I rolled him over and he had his hand on his side. I also saw blood drenching one of his legs.

"Menace, you were hit."

"Its ok." He put his other hand up to wipe my eyes.

"Its not ok. Baby, you have a lot of blood coming out and.-" He started coughing and blood was coming out.

"Shit, shit, shit. Call Joakim and your mom." I told Taylor who was in shock.

"Ma, take my phone and call his mother. She'll call everyone else." She did like I asked and I heard her telling his mom what happened.

"Dynasty, I'm gonna be fine and when they take this bullet out and I wake up, you're gonna close the room door and ride my dick to release this nut I been holding in."

"Menace." Here I am a nervous wreck and he's cracking jokes.

"I'm gonna be fine Dy. Stop crying." He started coughing again and the ambulance could be heard getting closer.

"She's on her way. Taylor lets get you to the hospital." My mom helped her stand up and the EMT's started working on him.

"Dy, check on my sister." I put my head up and she passed out.

"FUCK!"

"What's wrong?" He must've panicked because his eyes began rolling and the EMT's moved me out the way to get him to the hospital. They wouldn't let me get in and pulled off before I could curse them out. Another ambulance pulled up and they took Taylor away. My phone was ringing from Joakim.

"Joakim."

"Tell me what happened." There was no hello or anything.

"Joakim, we were coming out the doctor's office and a black SUV came outta nowhere and bullets were flying. We were all ok. Menace went to check on Taylor and.-"

"Taylor? Why was she there?"

"She came with him." I didn't know if I should be offended or what.

"He told her to stay under his truck and came back to check on me and another black car came flying and shot him. He was hit a few times. There was blood everywhere."

"Was anyone else hit? Where's Taylor?"

"She's in an ambulance."

CLICK! He hung up and right now I didn't have the energy to call him back. My mom was following behind the ambulance Taylor was in and even ran the lights.

108

"Park right there." I pointed to an open spot and we both jumped out.

"Dy, you have to relax."

"I'm trying."

"Try harder. Menace and Taylor are going to be fine and they'll both be pissed if you're not." I took some deep breaths and tried to calm myself down.

"Are you ok, miss?" I heard and stared at a nurse coming in my direction.

"Yes, why?"

"You have a lot of blood coming from your foot." I glanced down and sure enough it was pouring out. She had me sit down, called a tech and took my shoe off. More blood came pouring out.

"Do you know there's a bullet in the side of your foot?" Me and my mom looked down and sure enough a hole was in it. My adrenaline must've been pumping, and I didn't notice it. The tech wrapped my foot up in a towel and carried me in the back.

"What the fuck is going on?" Joakim barked and everyone turned around. There were a bunch of guys and his mom and Ms. Thomas, came running in with tears coming down their face. I tried to ask the guy to let them come in the back but he kept walking. He said, I already lost too much blood and it was critical for me to be seen.

He put me in a room and a doctor came in asking a bunch of questions. The nurse asked for my arm and placed an IV in it. I hurried to tell them about my pregnancy before they started giving me medication. The doctor gave me the rundown of what was about to happen because the bullet couldn't stay in my foot, nor could I receive anesthesia. They put the monitors on me, gave me some Demerol to relax and that's all I remember. When I woke up my mom and Ms. Thomas were sitting in a chair talking.

"Where's Menace? Is Taylor ok?" I could hear the monitors beeping.

"She's fine. You have to relax."

"Where's Menace?"

"Still in surgery."

"Why? He was hit on the side and leg." They both looked at each other.

"Menace had a heart attack on the way. The doctors had to get his body calm before going in." I tossed the covers off my legs and tried to get up. I heard my door open and Joakim walked in. The look on his face told me it was about to be some shit. Ms. Thomas knew too because she stood up and so did my mom.

"I'm gonna say this once and I don't wanna hear anything else." I pushed the button to make my bed rise. I folded my arms and waited.

"Ever since you came in Menace's life there's been nothing but bad shit happening around him. I don't know if this is all because of you but I know my brother has never been shot at, before you."

"I find that hard to believe." I did. Shit, he was in the streets and I would be a fool to think nothing ever happened to him.

"Bitch, believe it."

"Whoa Joakim. You fucking know better." Ms. Thomas pushed him back.

"No, Ms. Thomas. He has some things he wants to say and I'm here for it. Continue." My mom was fuming.

"Shit was quiet and we never had reason to watch our family, the way we do now. You've managed to get my boy to fall in love and that's all good but when you get him caught up in shootouts, that's where I step in." I kept the flat expression on my face as he spoke.

"I never thought I'd say this but he was safer with Quana and she's had her share of drama but nothing like this."

"Listen, little boy. You are way outta fucking line. I don't give a fuck who you are." My mom was in his face. I moved the covers back off my leg and sat up. I couldn't stand and it only pissed me off.

"Ma, I got this. Are you finished?"

"After you leave here, stay the fuck away from him or it won't be Quana you have to worry about." He headed for the door.

"Hold up motherfucker." He stopped and turned around with hate on his face.

"You can make all the faces and threats you want, don't shit scare me." Fuck my foot. I stood and held onto the wall. I felt stupid tryna talk shit and I'm sitting down.

"You're hurt and it was scary hearing about him getting shot and then, Taylor passed out. I'd be mad too but I would never allow Menace, or even agree with him going in someone's room disrespecting anyone the way you have. You walk your lying, cheating ass up in my fucking hospital room throwing out threats, insults and demands about your brother and I get it. However, I'm not Quana and for you to bring her up in here, shows me you don't respect the relationship he and I have."

"Had."

"What?"

"Had. You weren't together."

"Fuck you Joakim. I hope Taylor never takes you back." He charged me and pushed me against the wall.

113

"JOAKIM REEVES! ARE YOU CRAZY?" Ms. Thomas and my mom were punching him in the back and anywhere else their hits connected.

"Shit." He let go and backed up.

"Stay away from him."

"After what you just did, I most certainly will but make sure you tell him why." He stared at me and the tears were falling down my face quickly. Not because he scared me but because all I saw was Jamal doing the same thing. When Menace yoked me up, I saw the love he had for me in his eyes and knew he wouldn't hurt me. It wasn't hard and more to make me get in the truck. When Joakim did it, all I saw was hate and anger. If he snapped any more, there's no telling what he would've done.

"Get the fuck out." My mom opened the door and he took one last look at me and left.

"Are you ok?" Ms. Thomas was checking over me. I still had the IV in my arm.

"I'm fine."

"You're not fine." My mom walked out and asked a doctor to come in and check me.

"Ms. Thomas please don't tell Menace."

"WHAT? Hell yes I am. Joakim should have never done that."

"Please."

"Dynasty."

"Ms. Thomas. They've been friends for years and I know this will tear their friendship apart. Maybe if I weren't pregnant it wouldn't be as bad but Menace will not take this lying down."

"He's gonna wanna see you Dynasty."

"He can come to me. I refused to be anywhere around Joakim again."

"Dynasty, you're asking me to be ok with the shit he did."

"I'm asking you to make sure they stay friends and brothers. I will never be the one who broke their bond. Please don't say anything." The doctor came in and I could tell she was struggling with what I asked. People will probably say fuck that, let her tell Menace. I would be all for it, if they weren't friends for years. I know he should've thought about that first but his emotions are running high for his boy and Taylor.

****

"Ok, Ms. Sutton, you can go home when you're ready." I had to stay the night for observations. Ms. Thomas came in the middle of the night to tell me Menace was outta surgery and resting. Joakim was in and out of his room and Taylor's. They made her stay because she passed out and come to find out she was dehydrated. I don't know how when her ass was always eating and drinking.

"I'd like to leave now. Can you please discharge me right away?"

"Sure. Just give me a few minutes."

"You have to see him before you go."

"Ma, I don't wanna run into Joakim and he's probably still asleep." She stopped me from putting my shirt on.

"Fuck Joakim, Dynasty. He can't tell you what the fuck to do. Matter of fact, let me call Menace mom and see if he's in

116

there." I shook my head because she wasn't listening. The nurse came in with discharge papers and a wheelchair. My mom asked if she could wheel me to the floor he was on. It wasn't a good idea but no one listened to me. We got off the elevator and went to the room the receptionist told us was his.

"Menace baby. You shouldn't be trying to get up. The doctor said the stitches on your side can bust if you move too fast."

"Why are you here Quana? Where is Dynasty?"

"Right here but it looks like you don't need me."

"He doesn't. Why you think I'm here?"

"What the fuck Quana?"

"Its ok Menace. Ma, push me a little closer so I know he can hear me." She did and stepped out.

"This is why it wasn't ok for you to check up on her after I whooped her ass." She gave me a fake smile.

"She feels like you're still comfortable being around her and whether you are or not, she has no problem showing up. Menace, I only came to make sure you were ok. I'm happy to know you are."

"What the fuck is going on? What happened to you and why weren't you here when I woke up? Quana, did you try and keep her from coming in here?" It was like he heard nothing I said.

"Menace, I don't know where the bitch was. Shit, I got a call you were shot and needed to be by your side."

"Who the fuck called you?" I knew it was Joakim and instead of her saying it, I stopped her.

"I called her."

"Dynasty, why would you do that?"

"Because as much as, I wanna believe you two are over there's still love and I'm not going to try and stand in your way any longer. If I could get up and kiss your cheek right now, I would. But my foot hurts too bad. Take care Menace." He tried to get up and the machines were going off. I wheeled myself out and my mom and the nurse came over.

"Dynasty?" I turned my head and Quana came out with a sneaky grin on her face.

"Why did you lie for Joakim?"

118

"You may not give a fuck about tearing up a friendship but I do."

"But.-"

"Take care of him."

"Oh, I will. And just so you know, he told me he loved me the other day." She played a conversation on her cell and she asked if he still loved her and he replied *Yup* without hesitating.

"Thanks Quana. I needed to hear that."

"He and I will never be over and when you have his kid, I'll take very good care of it when we're together. I mean, he'll definitely wanna get me pregnant now."

"Goodbye Quana." I know she was trying hard to make me break and inside I already did. Once the elevator opened, Joakim stepped off with Taylor and their mom.

"Where are you going Dy? Did Menace see you?"

"Yea. I came to say goodbye."

"Goodbye. Why would you be saying goodbye?"

"I'm the reason all of this bad shit keeps happening to him. If I stay away, he'll be safe."

"WHAT? Dynasty, none of this is your fault. Why would you blame yourself for someone shooting at us? None of us could've predicted that."

"That's what I thought until someone told me otherwise." Joakim was staring a hole in my head and Ms. Thomas had her arms folded, looking at him.

"Besides, he has the right person in there with him now. Right Joakim?" She looked at him.

"He's been asking for you since he woke up so whoever's in there, don't mean shit."

"If only that were true." I asked my mom to press the elevator again because the doors closed.

"Take care Taylor and if I weren't scared something would happen to you, I'd invite you over. I'm sure Joakim agrees with me about us keeping our distance." His rage was growing and I could tell. The nurse backed me in and I could see Taylor trying to figure it out.

"Goodbye." I waved at the same time the doors closed.

"I just wanna smack the hell outta him." My mom was pacing the elevator.

"Its ok ma. We'll see each other again." It was true because Taylor asked me to not only be the Godmother but be there when she delivered. I don't know if I'll be in the delivery room but I had no problem being the Godmother but I know Joakim did. Oh well, not my problem.

Taylor

"What's going on and why is Dynasty talking like that?" I asked my mom and Joakim who both seemed to be in their own thoughts after she left. He shrugged his shoulders and my mom walked ahead of us.

"GO QUANA!" I heard Menace yell. I hurried to walk in the room and Joakim held me back.

"Don't go in there acting a fool. That's their shit."

"But why is she here? He don't even like her."

"That's his shit Taylor."

"Joakim, what's going on? You can't stand her either and now you're telling me to leave it alone."

"Nothing. I don't want you stressing yourself out with my baby." He rubbed my stomach and placed a kiss on it.

They brought me in the hospital because I passed out after seeing my brother shot. I went into shock and I guess my body shut down on me. I didn't hit the ground but I did fracture my wrist. Evidently, I fell as Dynasty's mom helped me up and she broke my fall but my hand was twisted under her. I was

122

dehydrated and they made me stay overnight to make sure I had enough liquids in my body. Now, here I am at my brothers' room door and his girl left, and his ex was in there. I know something is up and it'll come to light soon enough.

"Taylor, did you see Dynasty?" Menace was trying to get dressed.

"She left. What's going on and why is she here?"

"Evidently, Dynasty called her here." I saw Joakim put his head down and my mom sucked her teeth.

"Can everyone give me a minute with my brother?"

"Taylor."

"Joakim please." He left the room aggravated and I saw the way my mom stared at Quana. I closed the door and pressed the nurses button for someone to come in. Menace was bleeding from the side.

"Menace what happened when Dy came in here?"

"I don't even know. She heard me yelling at Quana and then told me this is why I should've never checked on her, after she beat her up."

123

"I agree because now Quana feels comfortable coming up here."

"That's what she said. Taylor, you know I don't want her."

"I do but why would she call her to come see you?"

"I don't know which is why in need to get outta here and find out."

"Hi. Can I come in?" The doctor asked and closed the door behind him. He looked at Menace side and removed the bandage. He said the stitches weren't busted but ne need to take it easy because they will. After he left, we finished talking.

"Menace, she blames herself for you getting shot."

"WHAT?"

"She said ever since she came around bad things have been happening and if she stays away maybe it won't."

"Why would she say that? I know someone shot her house up but we don't know if it was to get her or the people had the wrong house."

"I tried to tell her that but she wasn't tryna hear me. Are you sure she called Quana and how did she get her number?"

"I'm not sure of anything anymore. Taylor, she's gonna have my kid and I have so many plans for her. Why would she walk away? Maybe she didn't really love me. Fuck! We moved too fast." He laid in the bed and stared at the ceiling.

"Menace, she is madly in love with you."

"Then why isn't she acting like it? She left like I meant nothing to her."

"To be honest, I think something happened or was said and it pushed her away."

"But what? I haven't been with anyone and what could someone say to make her think this is her fault?" The door opened and everyone came in.

"We need to find that out." I turned around and Quana was coming in on the phone. I could tell by her conversation it was Candy.

"How many times did the baby kick?" I went to stand and Menace held me down.

125

"Goodbye Quana." My mom pointed to the door.

"I'll see you later Menace." She tried to make her way closer to him and I blocked her. Dynasty may not be here but she ain't about to do no grimy shit. When she walked out, I followed her.

"Why are you here?" She turned around.

"Why not?"

"He has a woman."

"You mean had. She left him and guess who still had his back?"

"Oh yea. Did you have his back when you cheated? Or spent his money on bullshit? What about not getting off your lazy ass to work?"

"Taylor, there's no need to be mad at me because the man you love couldn't keep his dick in his pants and brought a baby home. At least, if he gave you a disease you could get rid of it. A baby, not so much."

"How does it feel to know my brother gave a woman a baby, he just met. That has to hurt, knowing you tried many times for him to get you pregnant. He wants to have more with her and I'm sure he's gonna marry her."

"Ouch, that hurt a little but not as much as seeing your face, when Joakim can't stay from Candy's house once the baby is born. All she has to do is remove her clothes and he gives in. Men never could resist temptation."

"QUANA!" Joakim yelled out and she jumped.

"What? Don't come over here with that bullshit."

"Go home."

"Oh I'm going to see my best friend. She said the baby is kicking a lot. Should I tell her you'll be by again? I'm sure she'll be ready for you." The bitch winked and I grabbed her by the hair.

"You talk a lotta shit for someone who can't fight. Once I drop this load, I'm gonna beat your face in and Candy's too." I let go and she looked at my stomach.

"Oh, you thought she was the only one having his kid?"

"So, what you went and got knocked up to compete. Only dumb bitches do that." I moved in her personal space and Joakim grabbed my arm.

"She is the one who's competing, which is why she made sure he was fucked up to get him to give her a baby. But who has the house, the ring, a new truck and every penny in his bank account? Who is he with right now? Who is he whooping bitches ass over? Huh? You call yourself taking up for your friend when all you're doing is proving more and more, how petty and childish the two of you are. She will never win when it comes to him."

"Looks like she already has."

"Oh yea."

"Yup." She started walking backwards.

"You'll never have his first child." She stuck her finger up, opened the door to the steps and hauled ass.

"Tay, I told you not to get in it with her."

"Get off me." I snatched away from him.

"Don't get mad at me."

"Why not? Huh? She's right about her dumb ass friend having your first child. You're gonna be going to her place to see the kid. I guess, that's another thing I have to worry about."

128

"Nah, you don't." I don't even wanna know why he said that. I left him standing in the hall and went back in the room with Menace.

"Where's Joakim?"

"Who knows? Maybe he went to see his other baby mama." I took my shoes off and got in bed with him. I loved my brother and we always laid under each other when we were younger and every now and then as we got older.

"That's how you doing it Tay?"

"I'm not doing shit but stating the obvious."

"Yea but no one needs a reminder."

"Why not? I have one every morning when I open my eyes."

"What you want from me Tay? Huh? I've done everything to prove I don't want her and you're still not happy. If this ain't what you want anymore, tell me. I'm done tryna to fight for you and anytime you get mad, this is what I have to deal with. I fucked up, I did and I deal with it every day like you. But I'm not about to deal with this shit forever."

129

"I don't want nothing from you Joakim. Not a damn thing."

"Fuck this." He went to leave.

"I don't wanna be with you anymore Joakim." He stopped and turned around.

"You sure?" I wiped my eyes and shook my head yes.

"I wanna be with you but its almost time for her to deliver and its no telling what I'm gonna to deal with. I'd rather back away now and get used to living without you, then deal with another heartbreak."

"Oh, you wanna live without me now?" He came towards me and Menace sat up.

"Its for the best Joakim."

"Its best for who, you? Because I don't wanna be without you. You are the only woman I want and I can't tell you that enough. Its like we move forward and you let Candy or Quana get in your head and we get pushed back. You were gonna be my wife." He grabbed my hand and stared in my eyes.

"Tay, what the fuck you want me to do to make you stay with me? I'll do anything." I don't think he cared about the few tears falling down his face. At that very moment, I knew and felt how much he truly loved me.

"I… I…" I looked up at my brother and mother who were both waiting for me to answer. Honestly, I don't know what I wanted him to do. Nothing was making me happy or ok with this other baby mama shit.

"You don't want this Taylor." He pointed between us.

"Then its no reason for us to speak. Call me when you have a doctor appointment and go into labor. You'll get the same treatment as her from me. I'm fucking done."

"JOAKIM!" He stormed out and I wanted to run after him but my body wouldn't move. Maybe him leaving is the best thing.

"Let him be Taylor."

"Ma."

"You can't keep playing with his heart and feelings. One minute you want him and when those chicks come around, you toss him out again. Let that man be if you don't want him." I nodded my head and laid there until it was time to go.

Joakim

I wanted to murder Quana for bringing that shit up to Taylor. I was more mad, Tay entertained it. We spoke plenty of times about how they'd start some shit just because and she fell right into the trap. Then she said there was no more us. I love the hell outta Tay but I'm serious about leaving her alone. I can't keep trying to prove my love and she wanna believe what they say. The only way to make shit go away is killing Candy. I had no problem doing it. The only catch is she's still pregnant but I swear, she's gone after delivery.

I pulled up at the house and went straight to the shower. I had to figure out a way to find who did this shooting and why was Menace hit. I was dead wrong for treating Dynasty like that but it did seem like since they've been together, bad things have been happening. He's gonna have a fit when he finds out but I'll cross that bridge when I get to it. I washed myself up, stepped out and hopped in the bed. With all the running around and bad shit happening, I barely slept. I heard the alarm go off and stayed in the room.

"I'm not going to be here long." I didn't say a word and watched as she went in the bathroom. I heard the shower cut on, went downstairs to grab some water and sat on the couch. If she wanted to grab some things, I'd wait so I could lock up afterwards. I'm surprised she's here when she told me it was over.

"Joakim." I turned around and she had the nerve to be standing there naked. This is the shit I'm talking about. One... she knew my dick would get hard just by looking and two... she said we were no longer together.

"Tay."

"Come here Joa." I took a sip and stood.

"You're taking a long time." I felt like a kid who was about to get scolded by his mother.

"If you go see her again by yourself, I'll stab you." I made my way to her.

"If you even think about tryna be with someone else, I'll kill you." I smirked because I guess this was her way of saying we're going to be together.

"Tay, you are the only woman I want and if you don't want me, this has to stop." I licked my lips.

"So, you want me to find someone else to satisfy my needs?"

"Only if you don't mind dying." I placed a kiss on her belly and moved up to her neck. I bypassed everything else because the stairs were not the spot to make love to her.

"Joa, I'm sorry for going back and forth. I'm scared." I carried her up the steps.

"Scared of what?" I placed her on the bed and stared. Taylor, was beyond gorgeous and now with my kid in her stomach, she was even more beautiful.

"You wanting her after she delivers." I got on my knees and spread her legs open.

"Don't worry about that because I'm gonna kill her."

"Whatttt? Oh Shittttt." I latched on to her clit and felt it thumping in my mouth. I placed my index finger inside and she released her juices in my mouth. I loved tasting her and she knew because she made sure I stayed down there until she had at least four or five orgasms. My head game is the shit and so is hers.

"I love you Tay." I kissed up her body and sucked on each of her breasts. I bit down on her nipples the way she liked.

"I love too baby." Her hands were on my ass, as she pushed me inside. She wrapped her legs around my back and begged me to drill harder. No matter how deep I went, she never complained and a nigga loved it.

"Joa, please don't hurt me."

"I won't Tay. Shittttt." I had my hands on her hips as she rode me.

"Mmmm, damn I'm gonna cum Tay." I held her tight as she put that pussy on me. I can't even front. Some men say they have a woman with the best and it may be true, but hands down Taylor Thomas had the best I've ever encountered. She kissed my lips, then my chest, stomach and found her way to my man, who was down for the count. I was ready to go to sleep but she wasn't.

"Got damnmit." I moaned out when she used her mouth to make me cum again.

"You don't like it." She smirked and laid next to me.

"You know damn well I love it. Stop playing." She placed her leg on mine and snuggled under my arm.

"Why didn't you tell me?"

"I thought you would think I wanted it. Tay, I backed away, pulled my clothes up, cursed her out and left. If curse, she edited that part out. When I said you were it, I meant it." She ran her fingers in circles on my chest.

"No more leaving me Tay." She put her head up.

"No more leaving you Joa."

"And to prove it, we're getting married in the morning."

"Ok." She didn't even protest and that shocked me. Maybe she is ready to be with me forever.

****

"We did it." She smiled at me when we walked out the courthouse. If you're wondering how we did it so fast, that's easy. We planned on getting married in two weeks and were gonna make it a shotgun wedding. She wanted my last name before the baby came. Therefore; we had the marriage license already. She said, after you have the baby, the hospital automatically puts the moms last name on the crib and she didn't want that. And just like a man in love, I gave her what she wanted.

"Are you happy?"

"I am Joa. I really am." She wrapped her arms around my neck and the two of us stood there kissing on the street.

"I fucking love you woman." I lifted her up and carried her to the car.

On the way, I noticed some guy watching us. I put her down, had her get in and made my way to him. The closer I got, he smirked and walked backwards. He ended up running away and jumped in some black car. I couldn't help but wonder if it's the same one who shot at Menace and if Taylor was the target because no one else was here. *Shit, am I the target?*

"Where did you go?"

"Someone was watching us." She grabbed my arm and showed me her phone.

Unknown: *So you married that nigga. I told you what our plans were and you went against what I said. When I get a hold of you, they'll be hell to pay.*

"Its him."

"Who is this from?"

"Donnell. He said, that he and I, were getting married and would have a baby to make you feel what you did to me. Joa, he's going to kill me."

"Tay, I'm not going to let anything happen to you. Ok." She nodded her head.

"Let's go see your brother at the hospital and fill him in, on what's going on."

****

"So, let me get this right." Menace was rubbing his temples and Quana was in the corner tapping away on her phone. Maybe it was a bad idea to have invited her. I was so mad at Dynasty, I messed up and I see it now.

"You two fools got married without me and ma, and the crazy nigga following y'all."

"Pretty much and why is she here Menace." Taylor never had an issue addressing shit. I loved and hated it, only because she won't have an issue beating her ass while she's pregnant.

"Man, I woke up this morning and the bitch was tryna suck my dick."

"Yoooooo." I laughed hard as hell, while Taylor had her nose turned up.

"Really Menace?"

"Shit, you were. It did feel good for a minute but its because I thought Dynasty was here. I opened my eyes and my dick went soft." I had to make my way to her house and apologize.

"You ain't shit Menace."

"I told your ass not to come back but you did anyway."

"You can leave now." Taylor was standing in front of her.

"I'm not going anywhere." My wife looked at me and smiled. Before I could stop her, she snatched Quana up by the hair and literally drug her out the room.

"Ima beat your ass if something happens to my baby."
She closed the door and came over to sit on my lap.

"I see that crying shit works bro."

"What nigga?"

"Shit, your ass was shedding real tears for my sister and now look. She done let your ass wife her up. Maybe I should do some shit like that for Dy." I looked at him.

"Nahhhhhh. I ain't tryna marry her yet."

"Bro, I have to tell you something." He sat up.

"The day you were shot, I came to the hospital and.-" My phone vibrated and it was Candy telling me she was in labor.

"Lets go." I grabbed Taylor's hand and told Menace we'd be back.

"Baby, what's wrong?" I was basically dragging her.

"She's in labor." She stopped and let go of my hand.

"I will carry your ass up there if you don't come on."

"Joa, I don't think it's a good idea." I placed myself directly in front of her and made her look in my face.

"You are my wife Taylor Reeves and we are in this together." She nodded and pecked my lips.

"She got one time."

"One time and you can do whatever you want, when she has your stepdaughter."

"A girl, huh?" She had a smile on her face.

"Yea. I haven't thought of a name yet. What you got?" I pressed the elevator and waited for the doors to open.

"Joa. I would never name your child."

"Soon she'll be yours too." Her mouth dropped open but she knew not to speak a word. If I said certain things, she'd never question it.

We walked on the labor and delivery floor. I asked what room Candy was in and the nurse pointed. Taylor squeezed my hand and I stopped.

"You good?"

"Maybe I should wait out here."

"Not a chance. You need to be able to tell your daughter how she came into the world from your stomach with no problem."

"Joa."

"You ready?" She pecked my lips and we stepped in.

"HELL NO! SHE GOTTA GO!" Candy yelled and the doctor and nurse looked.

"Shut the hell up Candy." Her mom shouted.

"Ma, I don't want his whore in here." I could tell how mad my wife was getting.

"Whore? Never Candy. She's my wife." Her eyes got big and Taylor flashed her ring.

"What?"

"Shut yo stupid ass up and push my stepdaughter out so I can beat that ass, like I've been waiting to do for a very long time." I smacked Tay on the ass and she smirked. I knew she wouldn't forget me telling her to whoop Candy's ass soon as she delivered; afterbirth an all.

The doctor put the bottom of the table down, put Candy's legs in stirrups and told her to start pushing. At first, she refused because Taylor was in here but once those contractions kicked in, she had no choice. She was screaming, punching the bed, grabbing the railing and begging the doctor to take the baby out. That's what her ass gets for not accepting medication.

After three hours of her bullshit, she finally pushed my daughter out. She weighed six pounds, five ounces and was eighteen inches long. The nurses cleaned her up, handed her to me and I handed her to Taylor. I walked over to Candy and her mom gave us privacy.

"This is how shit is going to go." I grabbed her chin tightly and made her look at me.

"Your gonna sign these papers giving up your rights to my daughter." Taylor handed them to me. She kept them in her purse for this exact reason. We never knew when Candy would go into labor. At first, Taylor didn't agree with me taking the baby but after I told her, she may bounce with her, she had no problem.

"Joakim, please don't take my baby."

"What did I tell you in the beginning? Huh?"

"To leave Taylor alone and we could've co-parented."

"And you didn't listen. You even pulled that whack ass video of you tryna suck my dick out, at the baby shower to hurt her. The shit you pulled was uncalled for and I can't have my daughter around it. What if you decide to bounce with her? Nah, I can't and won't take the chance."

"Please Joakim." She pleaded and her mom walked out. Taylor put the baby in the crib and came over.

"Look Candy, regardless; of all the nonsense you put me through, I'm willing to let you visit and spend time with her."

"Why are you doing this? Is it because I had his first kid?" Taylor yanked her head.

"You may not see a child, but I am his first baby mother. You're just the one who pushed the first one out. Make no mistake Candy. This is my man, my husband and I will go to war for him and the baby. Now you can sign the papers and visit or he can kill you and there goes spending time with her."

"I don't want to."

"Not a problem." I picked my phone up.

"What are you doing?"

"Oh, sending a message for someone to come up here later and take your life. I can't do it because my wife will be fucking the shit outta me later."

"Hell yea I am." She smirked and my dick got semi hard.

"Plus, I need them to call me at home so I can play the sad father."

"Ok. Ok. Where do I sign?" I put the paper on her lap and pointed to the areas to sign.

"Can I hold her?"

"Absolutely. If you even think about doing some shady shit, I'll blow your fucking head off." She knew I wasn't playing. Her mom walked in with a smile on her face.

"Did she sign?" Oh yea, her mom is the one who helped me get a judge to sign off on the paperwork. She was sleeping with him and said her daughter was unfit. She even brought him photos of her partying before she got pregnant. He didn't know and as a man who upholds the law, he had to do what was in the best interest of the kid. Say what you want but my daughter will be protected.

"Ma, please tell me you didn't have anything to do with this."

"I had everything to do with it. You don't deserve this child and I hope no one else gets your pregnant." As you can tell, they don't get along and her mom couldn't wait for this to occur. She wanted me to do it sooner but I objected in case she really tried to bounce before having the baby.

"Can I have a minute with Sade?"

"Who the hell is Sade?" I asked and Taylor smacked me on the arm.

"Baby, its what she named her."

"I didn't agree to that shit."

"Stop Joa. It's a pretty name for a beautiful baby." She pulled me to the corner of the room because neither of us were leaving. I don't give a fuck how mad she was, this is happening whether she wants it to or not. My daughter started crying and Candy tried to breastfeed. I cut that shit short.

"Bitch, are you crazy?"

"Joakim, this is the best for babies."

"Nah, she'll be on formula. You think, you're slick bitch." I walked over to her.

"You won't get her hooked on breastmilk so you'll have to be around. Not a fucking chance. Open that fucking bottle." She sucked her teeth but did what I said and guess what. My daughter was fine with that. She better get the fuck outta here with that sneaky shit.

"Baby, I'm happy for you." Tay sat on my lap.

"I'm glad you're here because I'd probably kill her by now." She laughed.

"I thought you were gonna beat her ass."

"I am eventually. I know you would kill me if I laid hands on her and something happened to our kid." I rubbed her belly. She was four months now and the small pouch was poking out a little. I couldn't wait until it got bigger.

"Long as you know. I promise, you can beat her until she dies afterwards."

"I just might do that." We started kissing and you could hear Candy suck her teeth.

"Is there a problem?"

"No."

"I didn't think so. Hurry the fuck up and change her, so her real mom can hold her."

"Joa."

"Fuck her. I'm not sugar coating shit. You are going to be her mom, now that she signed these papers so she may as well get used to hearing it." I don't care how mad she was. I meant that shit about Taylor being her real mom. Candy, will be dead soon so everyone may as well get used to saying it too.

Dynasty

"Oh my God mommy. I did it. I finally got my license."
We were at the DMV waiting for them to process my
information to get them. After everything that's gone down, I
figured it was time for me to get my L's and a car. Taking an
Uber is ok but I wanna come and go when I want to, without
waiting on someone to pick me up.

"Its about time dammit. Shit, I didn't think you even
wanted them."

"Ma. Really?"

"I'm serious. You never said anything."

"That's because it was a surprise and you still wouldn't
have known, if I didn't need you to teach me." I shrugged my
shoulders and went to the booth where the lady called my
name. I took my permit test two weeks after I got home. Jen
helped me but I never mentioned it to anyone. The actual
driving test had to wait a couple months, due to the amount of
people getting their license and today was the day. I was so
excited and begged my mom to let me drive home. I still feel

like a kid sometimes when it comes to her. I guess because I missed so much time.

"Looky here now." I walked away from the booth and flashed the license in front of her.

"Girl, move." She laughed and stood up.

"Keys please." She sucked her teeth.

"I swear, you better not crash my shit." She brought a brand-new Kia Sorrento and it was nice as hell. I could've gotten one but until my license were in my hand, I refused.

"Why the fuck do I keep running into you?" Quana said outside of DMV.

"Because you're a got damn stalker." I started walking.

"I hope you know, Menace and I are back together."

"Oh. You mean after you tried to suck his dick in the hospital while he was sleep, he still wants you?" Her mouth fell open. The other day, Taylor, Jen and I went out to eat for lunch. It was to talk about the bridesmaid's dresses and other things. Jen was getting more excited for the wedding that was in less than six months. Never mind she and I, cursed Taylor out for jumping the broom and not telling anyone. Not that I would've gone but still.

"Whatever. You'll never have him boo. This pussy right here, keeps him stuck." I looked at my mom and we both busted out laughing.

"The same pussy he wouldn't dare put a baby in? The same pussy that couldn't get a job and became a boring fuck? I doubt it." I pressed the alarm and opened the door. This bitch had the nerve to run up on me.

"Hell fucking no." My mom came over.

"Bitch, my daughter won't beat your ass again because of my grandbaby but I'm right here. You wanna get your ass beat out here in this parking lot, I'm down but you won't touch her."

"I got you later Dynasty."

"I'll be waiting boo." I blew her a kiss and closed the door.

"What the fuck is wrong with her?"

"She misses Menace. I understand but she is overboard with her shit."

BOOM! I heard when we were backing out. My mom looked out the back window.

"Change seats."

"What?"

"Change seats. NOW!" We hurried to swap spots. Thank goodness, my stomach wasn't big because this would've been a lot harder. Me and my mom stepped out the car and I couldn't believe the drastic measures this bitch was going through. Quana was on the fucking ground screaming about being hit. I mean, she was hysterical with it too.

"You have to be kidding me." People started to come out of DMV and offer assistance, The cop inside came over and asked what happened.

"Oh my God, I think my back is broke?" Quana yelled and I turned my head to laugh. I picked my phone up and called Taylor to fill her in on this shit.

"I know you lying." She was cracking up on the other end of the phone.

"Girl, I'm about to send you a video of the shit she doing." I hung up and recorded her. Quana was screaming about her back and even said she think her leg was broke. I've seen some bad acting in my life but this was by far, the worse. I don't think the cop or EMT's believed her either. When they put the back board under her, she let fake tears fall down her face. Once they put her on the gurney she was begging someone to call her boyfriend Menace Thomas and that was it. I had, had enough of her bullshit. I waited for the cops to take our statement and got in the truck.

My mom and I drove to the house in silence. She could tell I was pissed and I could tell she was, too. The cop gave her a ticket for reckless driving, and said to fight it. The guy from DMV is supposed to call her later and explain what he sees on the video, which is probably why the cop told her to fight it. I'm telling you they didn't believe her ass either. She was doing too much for someone who had a broke back and whatever else she was claiming.

My mom pulled in the driveway and there was a burgundy colored Audi truck with a big red bow on it. I looked at her and she smiled. I stepped out and ran over to it, only for the door to open and Menace step out.

"Congratulations ma." I jumped in his arms and we started kissing. I think we both missed each other.

"Ummm. I'll see you in the house." Neither one of us responded and my mom left us out there.

"You missed me huh?" He put me down and stared at me.

"A lot. You miss me." I pointed to his hard on.

"Hell yea. You were supposed to release my nut, after I came outta surgery." I turned away and started looking in the truck.

"What's going on Dynasty? What happened and why did you leave?"

"It doesn't matter. You're ok and I checked on you everyday through Taylor. Did you buy this?" I changed the subject.

"Yea. Your mom told me about your test so I had it delivered."

"But how did you know I would pass?"

"Shit. The way you drive this dick, I knew you wouldn't have a problem."

154

"I can't with you right now." He rubbed my stomach.

"Did you eat?"

"No. I'm hungry though."

"You wanna take this for a spin and get something?" He saw the smile on my face and walked slowly to the other side.

"Menace are you supposed to be out the house?"

"No but who cares. Two weeks is too long and I needed to see you. You weren't answering my calls or text messages." I pulled out the driveway.

"Seeing her there really hurt me and.-"

"Why though? You called her." I could feel him staring. How could I answer without telling him the truth? I couldn't.

"You know what? Let's forget that part of you being in the hospital. I'm glad you're ok."

I drove to the closest diner and the two of us sat in there for two hours eating, talking and being nasty when no one was looking. I told him about the shit with Quana at DMV and he just shook his head. He told me about Taylor getting married, the crazy man watching them and how he went to Quana's

155

house and told her he loved her. I mentioned her letting me listen to him say it and he played a recording of his own. I could hear him saying he loved her in a friend way and I was who he wanted. You heard her begging and pleading for him to take her back. I was pissed she made me believe they were something, they weren't. I asked how he recorded her. He said, she was up to something when she started asking questions.

After the shit with Taylor, he didn't wanna be caught up in a web of lies. He knew she would try some sneaky shit and he was right. Quana even kissed him and he pushed her back. I had no reason not to believe him when he came out on his own to tell me everything.

It made me look at him in a different way. Maybe, all men are different. He wasn't trying to hurt or play me and I could see it clear as day now. He wanted more for me and I did too but it was hard when people from my past were trying to bring me down. Quana hated me because of him and her brother. She tried her hardest to keep us apart with lie after lie, but it didn't work. Ruthie revealed a son and an affair, I didn't know about. Yea, it happened a long time ago but it still hurts to know she was never my friend. We did everything together and to know she stooped so low, is a smack in the face. I guess, everyone isn't always who they portray. I wish, I'd known sooner because I never would've been bothered when I came home.

"You coming in?" I asked and opened my door.

"HELL YEA! I brought you a truck, and fed your greedy ass. I deserve to be compensated."

"And you will be. Come on daddy." I grabbed his hand.

"Aww shit now." His smile always made me do the same. I locked the door and we heard music coming from my mom's room.

"Looks like they're doing what we about to."

"Really?" He lifted me up and walked me up the steps. Once we got in my room, he locked the door, stripped out his clothes and made me do the same.

"You're so fucking lucky we're here." He led me in the bathroom.

"Why is that?"

"Because you deserve for me to beat that pussy up until you lose your voice from screaming." I don't know why but that shit turned me on.

"Get in. I wanna fuck you with soap suds all over you."

"Ok, weirdo." He laughed but I got my ass right in.

****

"Mmmmm." I woke up to Menace kissing in between my thighs. We had so much sex last night, I thought he'd be tired. He did say, we would be making up for days. I guess he wasn't lying.

I felt his hand move my legs around his head and moaned in my pussy as he made my hips go up higher. He penetrated me deep with his tongue and the burning desire in me, overtook my body as I shook violently. The sensation ripped through me again and I could no longer yell out for him to give me time to breathe. I almost fell off the bed from how good it was.

He sucked on my clit again, as I rocked my hips over his mouth; feeding him more of my nectar. He began gripping my titties and moved up to kissing on my belly. My wetness

158

was seeping out and I wanted him to puncture my insides so bad, I thrusted under him and forced his dick inside me. We both moaned out in pleasure. I let my nails rip into the flesh of his back with no remorse.

His lips were now pressed against mine as he proceeded to give me the ultimate pleasure I was seeking. Each thrust felt as though he was stretching me open down there. He would pull out and drive himself deeper and I couldn't get enough. The experience was mind blowing and I promised myself never to let him go again.

"You feel so damn good Dynasty." He bit down on his lip.

"So do you baby." He asked me to get on top and I happily obliged to his request.

"Sssssssss." It was painful, yet; thrilling and pleasurable at the same time.

"Just like that Dy. Got damn, I'm gonna cum." He sat up against the headboard. I grabbed the top of it, stood on my feet and went up and down, hard then fast and repeated it. The two of us were drenched in sweat. We started kissing and his tongue moved at the same rhythm of his dick pounding in and out. Our bodies were in sync and that only clarified us, needed one another.

"You ready to cum ma?" His mouth was on my neck, as his hands caressed my breasts gently.

"Yes baby, yes." He thumbed my clit and it became even harder. It felt like I was gonna explode and he knew it.

"I'm cumming with you." I nodded my head and continued riding him. We were both reaching our peak.

"FUCKKKKKKK!" We both shouted at the same time. My head fell on his shoulder and he sat there with his head against the headboard.

"I love you Dynasty."

"I love you too baby. I love you so much and I don't ever wanna break up again." He lifted my head.

"When I say take a break Dy, it doesn't mean I want anyone else."

"I know that now."

"Good and I think that break was long enough." He kissed my forehead.

"It was too long." He ran his fingertips up and down my back. I heard the doorbell ring and threw some sweats and a shirt on.

"You better not have another nigga coming over." I turned to look at him.

"Why not? He may be better than you."

"Yea ok. Play with me if you want." I blew him a kiss and told him, I'd be right back. I walked down the steps and saw Taylor through the peephole. She didn't look happy and I figured out why when I opened the door. Joakim was standing there looking like a kid who got in trouble, which only told me, he said something to her about what he did.

"Hey boo." She kissed my cheek and walked in. She took the baby from Joakim and made her way in the living room. Taylor was extremely happy to be Sade's stepmom and I loved to see her that way. I think everyone did after all the bullshit.

"Why are you here?" I folded my arms.

"Look Dynasty. I came to apologize for what happened because I was dead wrong."

"Ummm, right now is not a good time for this." I looked up at my room and the door was opened but he must've still been in the bed.

"No. Now is the perfect time. Its been a couple of weeks and.-"

"He just told me yesterday and I made him come over here." Taylor yelled from the living room.

"Its fine. Can we discuss this another time?" I didn't want Menace to hear. My worst fear is them fighting over the shit he did and said to me, and them not being friends.

"Nah. My wife said it had to be today."

"Joakim."

"I should've never put my hands on you or accused you of being the reason bad shit happened. I apologize and.-" I didn't even have to turn around to know Menace had either come out the room or was standing at the top of the stairs. The look on Joakim's face told it all. He wasn't scared but he had the, *I know, I fucked up look* on it. Shit, hit the fan from there.

Menace

I got up to use the bathroom when Dynasty went to answer the door. I ended up brushing my teeth and washing my face while I was in there. I came out and she still wasn't back in the room. It made me nervous because no one knew where she lived and the only friends she had, were Jen and Taylor. Imagine my surprise when I heard Joakim's voice. I couldn't make out what he was saying in the beginning because her room is upstairs, down the hall and away from the door. Me not knowing, started walking towards the steps and you couldn't see me because her room came from the opposite direction of the door.

I heard Taylor yelling about her making him come to apologize but what was he apologizing for? I could also hear Dynasty telling him, to come back another time. In my mind, whatever he was apologizing for, she didn't want me to know about. When I heard him mention the shooting and hospital, I stood there listening but when he said he put hands on her, I was livid and came storming down the steps. Taylor jumped up and Joakim looked me straight in the eyes. Dynasty never turned around but she knew, I was there.

"Menace, calm down." Taylor moved in front of me and Dynasty was crying.

"Move sis."

"Menace, he apologized." Dynasty stood on front of me.

"Then why are you crying?" I still had my eyes on him.

"Because I don't want you to fight over it. You've been friends for a very long time and." I leaned down, kissed her lips and pushed her to the side. I appreciated the fuck outta her for trying to keep us from fighting.

"Did you put your hands on her?"

"Menace."

"Did you put your hands on her?"

"I was mad and.-" I didn't even let him finish and hit his ass so hard, he fell against the door.

"Did you call Quana to the hospital, to piss her off?" He didn't say anything, so I hit his ass again.

"Did you blame Dynasty for the shooting?" I gave him a gut punch to the ribs and he hunched over.

164

"Menace, please stop." Dynasty yelled out and I hit him a few more times.

"If you ever put your hands on her again, I'll fucking kill you." I hit him in the face one last time and split his eye open. Not once did he attempt to fight back. Don't get it twisted. Joakim is deadly with his hands too but he knew his ass was dead wrong and didn't even attempt to hit me back.

"Menace, that's enough." Taylor came over with a rag and put it on his eye. Dynasty stormed up the steps and slammed the door. I helped Joakim up and walked him to their truck. Taylor asked me to keep Sade until they came back from the hospital. He was definitely gonna need stitches.

"I fucked up."

"You did and this is the only time, I'll forgive you."

"Love you bro." He and I hugged. This isn't the first fight we had but it's the first one where he knew I would never forgive him, if he did it again. I don't play when it comes to my woman and I'm sure he was hurt about the shooting but he went too far.

"Love you too. Taylor, let me know when you on your way back." She nodded and started the truck.

I waited for them to leave and went in to check on Sade. She was up whining a little. I opened the baby bag, took a bottle out and went to give it to her but Dynasty's mom took it out my hand. She said, it had to be warmed up. How the hell was I supposed to know that? She took her from me, changed her diaper and fed her. After she burped, I took her and was about to go upstairs.

"Take it easy on her Menace."

"She should've told me."

"I know but look at it from her point of view."

"I did and it still doesn't make a difference. Friends or not, she's pregnant and he had no business touching her." She nodded her head.

"She didn't wanna be the reason you two stopped speaking or broke up a friendship, you two had way before she came in the picture."

"The only people who can ruin our friendship/ brotherhood is he and I. That right there is a deal breaker and if it happens again, we won't speak. Its about respect and even though Taylor is my sister, I would never put my hands on any woman he was with, no matter what the situation."

"I understand."

"Good. Let me go make your spoiled ass daughter understand."

"She's stubborn."

"You don't have to tell me." I winked and went up the steps. I heard music playing and walked in the room to see her coming out the shower.

"Oh my God! She left her here." She reached for Sade and the towel fell.

"I'm gonna take her to your mom because you're about to make my dick harder than it already is." She laid Sade on the bed and rushed to put clothes on.

"You're not getting nothing from me." I sat her down on my lap and made her face me.

"I understand why you didn't wanna say anything but it wasn't fair to me."

"What you mean?"

167

"You left me in the cold because of the shit he did and said. I tried calling and texting and you left me at the hospital with the crazy ex. What would you have done if I fucked her or even let her suck my dick? Huh?" She sucked her teeth.

"Exactly! He was dead ass wrong and whether I was your man at the moment or not, it was my job to handle it and I would have."

"But you've been friends for a very long time."

"And?"

"And, I didn't want you to stop."

"That's for me to deal with, not you. Don't ever keep no shit like that from me again. Do you hear me?" She told me yes and picked Sade back up. I stared at how gentle and loving she was and couldn't wait for her to have our baby. She was gonna be a good mother.

Sade ended up staying the night with us because Joakim stayed at the hospital all night. He had some cracked ribs and ten stitches in his eye. They gave him pain medication and he went straight to sleep. My sister told me she had no hard feelings towards me because she too said he deserved it.

168

She agreed as far as, him knowing better and would lose his mind if the shoe were on the other foot.

My mom called me and said she was happy I found out because it was killing her to keep the promise for Dynasty. Evidently, she was there when it happened and my girl basically cried and begged her not to mention it. It took her a few minutes but she agreed, thinking it would've come out a lot sooner. She too said Joakim was owed that ass whooping. She cursed him out a few times over what he did and told him to come clean. Now that I think about it, I wonder if he was about to tell me that when Candy went into labor. I guess, it doesn't matter now.

****

"Are you sure it was Block?" I asked Valley who was in the office with me and Joakim.

"Positive. He had someone with him though. I couldn't see exactly who it was but by the frame, it appeared to be a female. Joakim and I looked at one another.

"Ruthie!" We both said.

169

"That's what I thought, until another one came out to assist."

"Wait! It was three people?"

"Yea."

"Fuck this. Show me the video." I sat back as he turned the video on, on my laptop. We had cameras in the warehouses, and on the trucks.

You saw the driver and two of the workers loading the truck with boxes of product. They pulled the back down, locked it and the driver and one of the workers jumped in the front seat. You saw them driving to the destination. I had him turn the volume down because their conversations were between them. The only time I listened, is if it benefitted me.

Shit, I had so many workers, I couldn't even tell you who this guy was driving or which spot he was about to go to. That's what I had people like Valley for. He wasn't always a top lieutenant. He got that spot when he showed his loyalty to Block and didn't tell when the trap house caught fire. He took that ass whooping like a champ too.

The driver parked in the back of a business and that alone pissed me off because it meant Block knew this was one of the trucks that carried weight. He knew a little about the business but not a lot. We watched the driver and worker get out, go to the back and open the door. One of them, rang the doorbell and waited.

See, we had it where, the product was brought in through the back like freight so no one would suspect anything. Shit, they usually sold out within a week an it's the reason why I sold more weight than the bullshit nickel and dime bags. I only did that for the youngsters coming up, trying to make money.

We continued watching and outta nowhere Block who had no fucking mask on, came running with a small ass gun and must've told them to put their hands up because its what they did. You saw someone close the door to the truck and jump in the front. The first thing the person did was hit the camera with a rock, breaking the screen. You couldn't see from the inside. They made a stop and once the back door opened again, the other camera clicked on. Two people turned into three. I asked where the truck was and Valley told me by the time they got to it, Block and his assailants were gone. I was pissed but not too angry. It only showed me that Block was still mad he got his ass beat and I got his woman.

"What you wanna do?" I poured myself a shot.

"Can't do shit with no leads."

"How do you think he found out about the stop?"

"The way is see it is, Block knew the days and some of the drop-offs. He must've been staking out all the spots and got lucky. Make sure the days of drop offs are changed ASAP." Joakim said and kept rewinding the video.

"I'm not worried because one of two things are gonna happen." They looked at me.

"One… his dumb ass will get caught tryna sell it. Or two… he's gonna try and get rid of it."

"How is he gonna do that?" I smiled.

"He's gonna go around in different areas asking to speak to whoever is in charge. He'll ask to set up a meeting and even charge the person a lower price. In return, the person will contact me and ask if I'll lower my prices because he's found competition. The shit will lead me straight to him."

"Do you think he's that stupid?" Valley asked.

"He's definitely that stupid. Hell, he thought with his cousin fucking the boss he didn't have to work and you see how that went."

"Yea. I can't believe we were cool. Who knew he wasn't loyal?"

"Never trust a motherfucker you didn't grow up with and even then, you have to keep your eyes open." I told him and stared at the camera. Dynasty and Taylor were here for some reason.

"You have to keep your eyes on him?" He pointed to Joakim who left the room to get the girls.

"Never. We may argue and fight but that's one nigga, I wouldn't ever worry about crossing me. Plus, my sister would kill him, an we all know how strung out he is over her."

"Hell yea. People wanna know how he's so hard in the streets and a damn teddy bear with her."

"Its how you're supposed to be. Jen got yo ass almost the same." He smiled and told me not to forget his bachelor party coming up.

"Hey baby." Dy came over and hugged me.

"Hey lil mama. What you doing here?"

"Taylor wanted to take her husband to lunch, so I came to see if my play one, wanted to go."

"I'll show you a play husband when you about to cum and I stop." I whispered.

"You play dirty."

"You have no idea." I stuck my tongue in her ear.

Valley shook his head and told us he'd see us later. Taylor and Joakim, shut the door and went into his office. I went to lock the door and Dynasty was sitting on my desk with her legs open. She was fully dressed but that pussy print was clear as day in those leggings. Needless to say, I had my lunch before leaving.

Block

"Can you believed we pulled that shit off?" I shouted when we got back to Candy's spot.

"What are we going to do with all those drugs?" Quana asked. Candy and I looked at her. She was already nervous about doing it and the whole time, complained and acted paranoid. Every cop we saw, she thought he was going to pull us over or that someone knew what we did and was going to tell. How do you live with a kingpin for five years and not be used to the street part of it? I understand he didn't have her around it but damn.

"Right now, we're gonna lay low."

"What if they know it was us?"

"They don't Quana, damn. Don't you think if they did, we'd be dead by now." She was biting her nails and shaking her leg.

"I could care less about them. Joakim took my daughter, so I took his drugs. Let's get this shit sold, do another hit and bounce out the state." She was more hood than Quana.

175

"You're gonna leave your daughter?" Quana asked her.

"I don't want to but I am never allowed to be with her alone."

"What you mean?" I sat back and listened to her talk.

"I'm allowed to see Sade three days a week and it has to be when Taylor is available. She will leave me alone with her and go sit in a corner to watch. There's also a big security guy who comes with her and even though I don't like it, I appreciate the gesture. After everything I did to her, I'm surprised she's doing this much. Anyway, I can tell she's taking good care of her too. Do you know my daughter wears Gucci outfits and she even had the shoes to match? I don't even have a pair of those." She went on and on about the different types of expensive clothing she'd see her and Taylor wear. You could see how jealous she was about not only Taylor raising the baby but the expensive shit the baby wore. It made me think Joakim did the right thing about taking her.

"Maybe you should leave her. You sound jealous as hell." Quana told her and they ended up arguing.

"YO! SHUT THAT SHIT UP!" Quana grabbed her things and slammed the door behind her. Candy took her ass in the bedroom. I locked the door and fell asleep on the couch, only to be awaken by someone sucking the hell outta my dick. I opened my eyes and Candy was devouring my shit like food.

"Shit girl. Suck it just like that. Mmmmm yea." I felt my nut coming up and put my hand on top of her head. I wanted to feel my sperm shoot down her throat. I loved for a woman to swallow.

"You like that Block?" She was being nasty and it only got my dick hard again. She removed the robe and climbed on top of me. Candy had a bad ass body and the way she was throwing her pussy on me right now, had a nigga lost. She was gushy, wet and moaning out, which drove me insane.

"Turn over." I could feel myself about to cum. I read somewhere if you change positions, it can stop it.

"Oh shit Block, you feel good. Fuck me harder." She spread her ass cheeks and started throwing her ass back. I smacked it and the shit jiggled.

"Yeaaaaa baby. Fuckkk." She moaned out and her juices were spilling out on my dick.

"That's sexy as hell Candy."

"Oh yea. I have something else sexy for you."

"What?" I was about to cum and wanted to see what she had in store for me.

"Try it in here." She opened her asshole and I indeed, gave her what she wanted. I don't know about other niggas but the tightness inside an asshole will make you almost cry out, from how good it felt.

"Ahhhhh shit girl." I played with her clit and a few minutes later we came together and fell on the couch.

"Go get me something to wash my dick off." She stood up and grabbed me with her. I had to catch myself from falling because my jeans and boxers were only at my knees.

"Its been a long time for me and we're about to fuck all night." She smirked and led me in the bathroom.

"Who said I wanted to?"

"This banging ass pussy I threw on you."

"Cocky."

"Confident baby. Now fuck me to sleep." I stripped out my clothes and the two of us definitely had sex all night. Her pussy was good as hell, so was the head. I don't know what Joakim was thinking getting rid of her. But I'm glad he did because I would've never had it.

****

"What Ruthie?" I answered as Candy sucked me off. For the last week, she and I had been out looking in other areas for someone to buy the drugs. Then we'd come to her house and fuck the shit outta each other.

"I'm coming in town next weekend."

"Ok. But stay outta sight."

"I know fool. Do you miss me?"

"Yup. I miss you a whole lot." Candy looked up at me smiling and took my balls in her mouth.

"Talk dirty to me on the phone Ruthie." She did and between her talking that nasty shit and Candy riding the shit outta me, I came hard as hell and fell straight to sleep. That was some sexy as shit to me.

After I woke up, Candy and I went by my aunt's house and noticed Quana's car there and another one I've never seen before. I called inside and there was no answer. I rode around a few times before stopping to go in. You would think Menace had someone watching her house but then again, he most likely didn't see her as a threat and assumed I was long gone. He would've been right, had I not fucked Candy. I was hooked on that sweet ass pussy.

We both threw our hoodies on and stepped out her car. Joakim had no reason to watch her either. That's what made the choice to put them on my team, a great idea. Menace and Joakim had no reason to suspect any one of them but little did they know. The hurt and pain they instilled on both of them, is the exact reason they should've been on it. I know, I would have.

I opened the door and heard moaning coming from one of the rooms. This bitch is really fucking in my aunt's house. I went in my room, shut the door and turned the music up. Candy laid on the bed and fell asleep while I was in deep thought of who could and would buy the shit. We had it in a storage unit for now and I didn't wanna leave it in there longer than thirty days.

KNOCK! KNOCK!

"What up?" I couldn't believe who was standing in front of my door in just a pair of shorts and a wife beater. A devious grin came across my face because here I thought Quana was being paranoid and about to fuck shit up. When she was a step ahead of me. If there's a motherfucker who won't be scared to go against Menace, this is him.

"Shit. What's up with you?" He lit a blunt and told me to follow him. My cousin was in the bed laying down. I saw her smirk when I walked past.

"What day you tryna hit him up again?"

"I figured we'd wait at least another two weeks. Give him time to think we left, but this time, I wanna get two trucks."

"That's being greedy. You already got one and from what Quana tells me, you wanted to hit one more time."

"I know but do you know how much money we could make?"

"Greedy niggas get caught Block. Think." He passed me the blunt and leaned on the side of the house.

"We'll go in another two weeks."

"Word!"

"Word! Let me get a few things situated and we good."

"That's what I'm talking about." We slapped hands and he went back in the house. That nigga Menace ain't gonna know what the fuck hit him.

Jen

I know y'all haven't heard a lot from me but its for
good reason. I'm a twenty four year old woman from Ohio and
I don't really have much of a story, besides being in love with
Valley, having his baby and about to marry him. We've had
our ups and downs like all relationships and yes Ruthie was a
downfall. But to be honest, I did some things while we took a
break as well. We know women can keep secrets, which is
exactly what I did and refused to tell anyone. However; that
exact secret has come back asking for compensation of some
sort to keep their mouth closed. I should tell Valley but then
he'd try and leave me. He's always said if he found out another
man touched me, he wouldn't be able to take it and I worked
too damn hard to keep us together.

If you can't figure it out, Valley was my first sexual
relationship but not my first boyfriend. He is the one who
broke my virginity and taught me everything in the bedroom.
Any time he wants a freak or decided to try new things, I'm the
one who supplied him with the fantasy between the two of us.

183

There was never a threesome and if that's what he wanted, I went on a website and showed him some. That's the closest he was to getting one because I wasn't ok with anyone satisfying him but me.

Anyway, the person found out about my upcoming wedding and began making outrageous demands. I'm talking about wanting to have dinner out in the open, have sex in local hotels, not that I'm with it. He wanted money and some other shit and said he would tell, if I didn't accommodate him. So far, I've done a good job at procrastinating but he was getting inpatient. Now, I could tell him to fuck off but it's a possibility he'd tell. If I went to be with him, it's a possibility he would still tell, so really, I had no win in the situation.

Then you had my ex Jesus, who came back from God knows where and requested my attention too. I don't know why, when we haven't spoken in years. The reason being is because the motherfucker was bat shit crazy. For a nigga who didn't get the pussy, he sure was coo coo for coco puffs and that's some real shit. Don't get me wrong. He was well mannered, sexy as hell, and a damn good kisser. Unfortunately, he was possessive, obsessive and downright dangerous. I had

to get a restraining order on him because he did some wild ass

shit to me. You think the dude stabbing Taylor in the hand with

a fork is crazy, let me give you a short story of what I went

through. Mind you we were only together for six months

before he went crazy.

We were on a date and some guy was looking at me

and smiled. Jesus must've seen him and thought I encouraged

it. Well this nigga got me to his place, started a bath and had

me get in. We had been out all day, so I'm thinking it's a nice

gesture. *Sheiiiittttt*. I was laying in the bath and he came in ten

minutes later talking about let me give you some fresh hot

water, since this is cold. I closed my eyes and heard him lift the

drain. The water began to drain and I got a little chill because

the water was going out.

I heard the bath start again and felt the hot water

coming out on my feet. Not even a minute later, I screamed

loud as hell. This nigga had poured a huge pot of boiling hot

water on me. I tried to get out and he pressed down on my

stomach and made me lay in there. He had gloves on his hand

so of course it didn't bother him. My skin was burning and I screamed until I had no voice. I had second degree burns on parts of my body and it took me a very long time to be comfortable with myself. To this day, I still won't take a bath if Valley's home unless he gets in at the same time.

Now that was enough for me to call it quits. But not with him. This nigga said we were in this forever and started stalking me. Wherever I went, he was there and the shit was scary. I ignored him, thinking he'd go away. Not a chance. This crazy man had a dozen roses sent to me at home, one day. Again, it was a nice gesture but we were through and I knew he wouldn't be in my future.

I opened the card and it read, *You'll never be rid of me. I'll be like a roach that won't die, no matter how many times you kill it.* I had no idea what he was talking about and tossed the card in the trash. I went to the doorbell that rang a few minutes after the flowers came. The delivery guy handed me a huge box. I was nervous about accepting it but the return address was from outta the country. I thought it couldn't be from him, if its from outta the country. I opened it up and there

186

was a box inside of it. When I opened the second one, I dropped it and both flying and regular roaches fell out. They were everywhere. I had them on my clothes, in my hair, they were crawling over my feet and anywhere else they could.

My mom didn't know why I was screaming, came in and pushed me out the door. She started knocking them off me and held me because I was shaking so bad and couldn't calm down. She called the police and once they came and saw the house full of that shit, they called all these different people in to get rid of the bugs. You would think an exterminator could do it but because there were flying ones, they needed someone else.

We had to move because I refused to go back in the house. I almost ended up in the psych ward because I had nightmares and felt like bugs were on me all the time and nothing was there.

At that moment, I had to file a restraining order. I had it sent to the last known address and he actually showed up at court. The judge asked if he did the things I said and he admitted to it. He gave me the restraining order and told him to stay away from me and not to send me anything else. It didn't make me a never mind because me and my mom moved to New Jersey, right after. Which is why, he couldn't find me but somehow, the punk popped up and has been stalking me again. The nightmares started and I won't even sleep until Valley gets home. Say what you want but being with a crazy nigga will scar you for life.

"Bitch, what are you daydreaming about?" Jen asked and picked Sade up. We were at the restaurant eating and waiting on Dynasty. We've been meeting up once a week to talk about the wedding. Yea, we can talk on the phone but its fun to meet up and we all loved to eat.

"Jesus, has been calling me and I'm scared because he tells me what I'm wearing sometimes." Her and Dynasty were the only ones who knew about him. Well, Valley knew of him but he didn't know what he looked like.

"Jen, Valley has a higher position now and being you're one of my best friends, I think you should tell him so he can protect you."

"What does his position have to do with anything."

188

"The higher the position, the more respect you get. These workers out here wanna be like Valley. They saw him come up and they want the same, which means if he puts the word out that someone is bothering you, they'll be on the lookout to catch him. Even though you may not know who the workers are, they will be familiar with you and if they see anyone bothering you, will have no problem stepping in."

"I don't know Taylor. He may think other shit."

"Jen, you didn't cheat on him. Shit, you did exactly what I did and gave him a taste of his own medicine. He may not know but that's the beauty in it." She always said, a man may not know his woman cheated but as long as she knew, its all that mattered. He'll feel like he has the upper hand until you pull that spade out at just the right time.

"I know but.-"

"Jen, you're driving yourself crazy for nothing. Whoever the dude is, obviously don't wanna tell because he would've done it already. I wouldn't even sweat that shit." I never told anyone who the dude was and planned on taking the shit to my grave.

189

"Yea, I guess."

"You still having nightmares?" I played with the salad, the waitress placed in front of me.

"A few times a week."

"Call your mom."

"She'll start worrying and I don't want that."

"Jen, its ok to be vulnerable sometimes. You don't always have to be the strong one." I nodded and smiled when I saw Dynasty coming in. Her and Taylor were a month apart in their pregnancy. Menace and Joakim, were excited as hell to be having kids together. It didn't stop the guys from coming to visit V.J and tell him about all the ho's he's gonna have when he grows up. Menace had the nerve to buy him a small basketball court already. My son isn't even one year's old yet.

"Hey y'all." She slid in the booth and asked where my son was.

"With his grandmother." His mom always had him. She thinks she slick. Her ass was at our house more than hers. I told Valley to go ahead and move her in but he said hell no.

"Ok, well he needs to come visit his Godmother. I have some new stuff for him."

"Dynasty, I told you not to buy him anything else. He has so much shit already." She waved me off and ordered her food. We stayed there for about an hour and went our separate ways.

I walked to my car and his scent was everywhere. I turned around and he was sexy as fuck. Valley was brown skin with a beard, that I loved tickling my pussy when he went down. You could see his muscle through his shirt and he could fuck me standing up for long periods of time. He put me in the mind frame of Larenz Tate and we all know he how sexy he is. he moved closer to me and my panties instantly got wet. The affect he had on me is ridiculous. That's why I was so hurt he cheated on me. To know another woman received the same pleasure, killed me.

"Why you out here by yourself?"

"My two best friends are right there pulling off." I pointed to their cars.

"And, I was waiting for my fiancé but since he's not here, what's up?" He smirked, lifted me up and sat me on the trunk of my car.

"You think he'll know if you gave me a taste?" He unbuckled his jeans and slid my dress over my ass.

"What he don't know, won't hurt him."

"I like that. Come closer." He moved me down to his exposed dick and ran it up and down my pussy lips.

"What else you like?" We looked around and the parking lot was vacant.

"I like the faces you make when I do this." He pulled my panties to the side and rammed himself inside.

"FUCK!"

"What's wrong?"

"You're bigger than my fiancé. Shit, he's definitely gonna notice but you're so worth it. Ssssss." I moaned out and bit my lip.

"I love you so fucking much Jen." He pulled my face to his and plunged in and outta me. The thrill of us fucking in the open was amazing and fun.

"I love you too baby.

"I'm just happy you didn't leave me for good."

"You ok?" I had him look up.

"I thought you would seek revenge for what I did and I'd have to kill you and him." I didn't know what to say.

"I'm too in love with you."

"I feel the same." We started kissing again and this time, it was more emotional than anything. What I mean by that is, I felt all the love he was speaking about in the kiss. I don't think he'd ever cheat again.

"Turn that ass around." He helped me down, placed my hands on the trunk and literally fucked me so good, I came at least four times.

"Make your fiancé cum." He whispered and I gave him what he asked for.

"You're gonna be pregnant off that nut." He smacked my ass, pulled my dress down and his clothes up.

"How can I explain that to my fiancé?"

"Don't. I got you baby for whatever you want." He opened the car door and stood in front of it.

193

"Meet me at the hotel up the street. I need to hear you moaning and your mother in law don't know how to go home."

I busted out laughing.

"You better not let her hear you say that." He kissed my lips and closed the door. He watched me pull off and came behind me. Off to the hotel we go.

Valley

I woke up before Jen and stared at her sleep. I was so in love with this woman that the thought of another man bedding her, made me sick to my stomach. When she found out about me and Ruthie, it broke my heart to see how bad it hurt her. She was hysterical crying, packed all her shit, left me and refused to talk to me for months. Gifts, flowers, candy, love notes, text messages, nothing was working, when I tried to get her back. When she said it was over, she meant that shit and I swore on my life, never to cheat again. My heart couldn't take that shit and I'm not ashamed to admit it. Too many men hide their feelings and its why they miss out on a good woman.

The day at the hospital when Ruthie shouted that bullshit, I knocked her fucking head off and wanted to do it again. Had Menace mom and sister not jumped in, I would've probably ended up in jail. Then I saw her out a few times afterwards and the bitch had the audacity to try and fuck again. I was so drunk the first time, I can't even tell you if the pussy was good or not. She said something to make my dick hard and not thinking, I took her to a hotel and went home, like a dummy. Not that I should've stayed out but I would have gone to my mom's or something. I'll never get intoxicated like that again.

I lifted the covers off my legs and walked in the bathroom to shower. Tonight, was my bachelor party and a nigga was walking down the aisle in two weeks. The party was early because Jen didn't want me having a hangover the next day. I haven't been drunk since the shit happened with that bitch and didn't plan on it tonight. However, she wanted to make sure I was ok if I did. She even told me to call her if I needed a ride. Not that I would but at least, she's got my back.

"Hey you." I heard her come in the bathroom. I looked out the glass door and she was sitting on the toilet.

"Hey. I was gonna let you sleep."

"Its ok. I miss V.J." I smiled because my son is definitely a mama's boy. He would try and get outta anyone's hand to get to her.

"And I miss his mama." She stepped in with me.

"Why do you love me Valley?" I turned to look at her and she was standing there with the most innocent look on her face.

"Because you are the woman who taught me how to love and appreciate you. You taught me, that your heart can't be played with like a game. You take very good care of me in more ways than one. You're not lazy and make sure the home front is good every day. You're the mother of my son, and you take very good care of him too. Last but not least, you are the only woman in this world I'm afraid of losing."

"Valley."

"I don't wanna lose my mom or other females in my family either but my love for them and you, are separate. I can't explain the feeling but know, I'll kill anyone over you and I don't care who it is. Your love is the only one, I can't fathom being without." I wiped her eyes.

"Why do you ask?"

"I just wanna make sure you're ready." I started washing her up.

"I made a vow to never cheat on you again and I mean it. I'm sure this bachelor party has you worried but let me be clear." I had her lift her legs up so I can wash in between her legs.

"There will be strippers and most likely my dick will get hard, but I promise not to allow anyone to touch me and vice versa. Well, I may smack some ass or something but you know what I mean." She laughed.

"But I will never disrespect you again and I apologize again for it."

"Is that good enough?"

"I love you Valley and I trust you. Its those heffas I don't. If you wanna fuck a stripper, you know I got you." She turned around and started twerking for me in the shower. That's what I loved the most about her. If I had a fantasy, she'd play it out for me. As far as, being a stripper, she's done that quite a few times for me and each time, we'd end up fucking like we were about to now.

****

198

"Damn daddy. You not only sexy but I feel that big ass monster you working with." One of the strippers said as she grinded on top of me. The bitch was sexy as hell and naked.

"DON'T DO IT NIGGA!" Joakim yelled and Menace was using his hand and making a sign under his throat saying the same thing.

"Awwwww, you worried about getting caught. I can keep a secret." She turned around, straddled me face forward and started kissing on my neck. It felt good, I ain't gonna lie but my girl means too much to me.

"Keep dancing but this is as far as, I take it. Sorry, I'm not losing my life for you." She sucked her teeth and basically rode the hell outta me, in front of everyone with my clothes on.

"Can you imagine what she'd do if y'all were naked?" Menace sipped on his beer.

"I'll take the imagination for a thousand. Jen won't be cutting this dick off." They both started laughing.

"Yo, what is Candy and Quana doing in here?" I pointed and both of them turned their faces up.

"Hold up! Is that who I think it is with Quana?" We looked and I had no idea who the dude was.

"Yup. That's him and it seems like they rekindled the fire."

"Good for him. Maybe she'll leave me the fuck alone now."

"I don't know about y'all but I'm about to touch all the ass I can, before I go home."

"Just make sure your digits don't slip in the pussy. Not every chick smells good." Joakim almost made me spit my drink out when he said it.

Throughout the night, different dancers came over and offered all types of sexual favors. I guess its true about women wanting what was already taken. The shit they offered was things most men fantasize about and here I have it thrown at me but the only woman on my mind, is my girl. As one of the girls danced on me, a familiar face came in view and I pushed her off. I could hear my name being called but I couldn't risk the nigga getting away. He must've noticed me coming because he took off. Don't ask how he knew who I was but it was ironic for him to leave when I walked to him.m

"What's up?" Menace was behind me with Joakim and a few other dudes.

"This guy who used to stalk Jen was here."

"Say what?"

"Jen used to fuck with this dude named Jesus and he became obsessive and crazy over her. He started taunting her and did some bad shit to her. She filed a restraining order and her mother moved her away because it was real bad. I couldn't find the nigga for years and I swear, he was just in here."

"Wait! I thought you were the only guy she was with." Joakim said, which let me know Jen mentioned her ex to Taylor.

"Sexually yes. She never got the chance to do anything with him because he got crazy. Fuck! If he's in town, it means he's gonna try and find her. I have to go." I ran back in to grab my phone and caught Candy opening the back door. I stood to the side trying to see who she was letting and wouldn't you know, it was Block and a few other niggas who all seemed to be strapped. I looked around the club and the shit was packed. I had no time to get Menace and Joakim attention. I saw a waitress walking by and grabbed her arm.

"Yo. Go tell Menace and Joakim, public enemy number one is here." She looked at me crazy.

"Bitch, go tell them and I swear if you don't, I'll find you later and slice your damn throat. Now hurry the fuck up." She ran off in the direction of where I left them. Block was walking to the VIP section and his so-called crew split up. I saw Menace and Joakim, pushing through the crowd and made my way behind Block.

"You got some fucking balls coming here." I put my gun on the back of his head. His hands went up and he turned around.

"Well, if it isn't my old best friend."

"Nigga, you snitched and tried to throw me under the bus when your ass fucked up. Best friend my ass." He put his hand down, pressed some button on his coat and there was an explosion by the door. After that, chaos broke out and people were running and screaming. I had my eyes on Block, who was making his way to the front. I pulled the trigger and watched his body drop. I made my way to the door and by the time I got there, he was gone. Blood was on the floor but his body was missing. I went outside and saw someone putting him in their car. I couldn't make out who it was and shot through the crowd again in their direction.

"Yo, where he go?" Everyone was outside with me by now.

"I definitely hit him but somebody helped him get away. I got the plate number though."

"Its all good. His time is coming. You good?" Menace asked and had security moving people out.

"GET HIM!" I pointed to one of the guys that came in with Block. I only knew it was him because they had the same shirts on. Some guy tackled him to the ground and carried him in the club. I don't know what the hell Block is tryna do but he's in for a rude awakening if he thought for one minute, I'll let him live after recently finding out, he stabbed me in the back, a year ago. That shit will never be ok with me.

Quana

"We have to get him to a hospital." I yelled out as Candy sped off from the club. The plan was to go in, scope the place out and leave. Don't ask me when or why, Block even came in. When we left Candy's house, he was still there. Not to mention, these so-called guys he had with him. Who were they and where did they even come from?

"You know they'll be looking at the hospitals."

"Take him to an Urgent Care. They can't deny him service, right?"

"I don't think so, but let's take him to one, a town over." I agreed and rubbed Block's face as he groaned in pain. He was hit in the back it seems like but you can't really tell. All I could think about was my brother dying and how I missed him say his last words.

KNOCK! KNOCK! The pounding on my mothers' door made me a little nervous because Jamal was in the streets and we never wanted to receive the call, that he was dead.

204

KNOCK! KNOCK! There it goes again. I sat there, while my mother came running down the steps. She looked at me and asked why I didn't get up to answer it. I had no answer for her and moved my legs, under my chin. In my heart, I knew something was wrong and once those two officers walked in, my fears were correct.

"Ms. Singleton, Ummm. I don't know how to tell you this but.-" The cops were well aware of who my mom and I were because Jamal made sure they kept an eye on us.

"What's wrong?"

"Ummm. Jamal and his girlfriend were…"

"I KNEW IT! I FUCKING KNEW IT! SHE KILLED HIM, DIDN'T SHE?"

"I'm sorry." One of the cops caught my mom as she fell into him.

"Where is he?" I asked and started putting my shoes on.

"It just happened so everyone is still at the scene. We came here first because of who he is. Are you ok?"

"Hell no, we're not ok. Ma, lets go." The cops escorted

her to the car, sat her inside and I hopped on the driver's side.

I didn't even wait for them to get in theirs and pulled off.

Jamal didn't live far from us so it only took us a few

minutes to get there. Police, EMT's, the coroner and media

were already on the scene. Caution tape was everywhere and I

wanted to get out but again, I was frozen. That is until, I saw

them bringing that stupid bitch Dynasty out. I told him to leave

her but nooooooo, he had to fall in love. No matter how many

times she told him to let her go, he wouldn't. Its like she had a

hold on him and he was the only one, who couldn't move on.

Yea, its been plenty of times my mom had to rescue her

from him. So what? Her mom went a few times as well but she

refused to watch her daughter go through the abuse and

stopped. Why didn't she talk her into leaving if it was that bad?

I've seen the marks, bruises and even knew about the

miscarriage but again, why didn't she leave? He wasn't

holding her hostage. I mean, she went to school and was about

to go off to college so how couldn't she leave?

"Are you ok Dynasty?" My mom asked when we got out the car and walked towards them bringing her to their car.

"I'm sorry, Ms. Singleton. I couldn't take it anymore. I found out about the baby on the way and he shot me. I loved him so much and if he would've gotten help..."

"I know baby. I know." My mom had the nerve to agree and hug her.

"Ma, really? She just killed your son, my brother and you're comforting her."

"Quana, I know you're hurting but I never meant for this to happen. He was going to kill me."

"AND!"

WHAP! My mom smacked the shit outta me.

"Don't ever let me hear you say that shit again. You know damn well how bad he was beating on her. I love my son with everything I have Quana but we both knew this day would come. Stop blaming her."

"She should've left him alone. Why didn't you leave? I HATE YOU! I FUCKING HATE YOU! I HOPE THEY BURY

YOU UNDER THE JAIL!" I started punching her and I know

she wanted to hit me back but the handcuffs stopped her.

"Stop it Quana." I saw the tears going down all of our

faces.

We stood there watching the cops put her in an

ambulance. Evidently, he did shoot her first. As they pulled

away the media was asking people questions and I was about

to answer them myself but stopped. Nothing could prepare me

for the coroner coming out with my brothers' body. I asked

them to let me see and at first, they didn't want me to. One of

the cops told them it was ok and as he unzipped the bag, I was

hoping it was someone else. I prayed it was someone else.

Jamal always said he would fake his death if the streets were

after him. But nope. It was indeed his body. I touched his face

and my mom stared down at him.

"Son, I told you to let that chile go. I love you son and

I'm going to miss you but you'll forever be in my heart." She

bent down to kiss him and broke down. No one ever wants to

lose their child and to see him dead is the worst thing a parent

could go through.

The following day, they had a hearing and you damn right I was there; bright and early. When she came out the cops had to stop me from jumping over the bench. I'm not a fighter and I've watched her beat hella bitches ass over my brother but she had handcuffs on and I knew she wouldn't be able to do much.

The judge denied her bail and she spent seven years behind bars. Now she's home and chaos is all around her. My cousin is shot, my man left me for her and my nephew still doesn't have his father. She doesn't deserve to live and I'm going to make sure she takes her last breath, soon.

"We're here." Candy stopped the car and ran to the door.

"Block, we're here. You ok?" He was barely breathing and the blood had drenched my clothes.

"Block, don't go to sleep. We're here now." The door flew open and a doctor and nurse asked us to help bring him in. It was late and there was no one there but the two of them. They questioned why we didn't go to the Emergency room and we said this was the closest spot. Once they got him in, it was a waiting game.

****

"Hi, Ms. Singleton." The doctor came out four hours later. It was now five in the morning.

"Yes." Candy and I stood up.

"Mr. Singleton, suffered a gunshot wound on the left side of his back. We were able to get the bullet out and stitch him up but he's going to need a physician who specializes in that."

"If you have the bullet out, he should be fine."

"Yes, but we aren't equipped to deal with the type of trauma he came in with. Therefore; we removed it and did what we could. However, he needs to go to a hospital, get x-rays and other tests done, to make sure the rest of his body is taken care of. And to be sure he doesn't have fragments left in him or anything wrong on the inside." Candy and I stood there listening to him tell us the effects of what can go wrong if he doesn't get to one. I took him up on the offer to have an Ambulance pick him up and take him to a trauma hospital. I asked if it could be one out of the area because the shooter may return. He agreed and not too long after Block was picked up and transported to one twenty minutes away. That wasn't far enough but it'll do.

"Take me home."

"You're not going to the hospital?"

"He'll be fine. I need to change clothes and tell my mother, who by the way is going to flip out."

"Maybe, I should go home and change too." We drove in silence and when she dropped me off, my mom was in the living room watching television. She was getting ready to leave for work.

"What the hell happened to you?"

"Block was shot and.-" She put her hand up to stop me.

"Why?" I shrugged my shoulders and she came towards me.

"You're out here running these fucking streets like you some big time gangsta bitch." I looked at her.

"Yea, I hear things too. Whatever you have up your sleeve for Menace, his girlfriend and whoever else, stop it. Its only going to put you next to your brother and I don't want to bury another child."

"Ma."

"I don't want to hear it. What hospital is he at?" She grabbed her things, told me to keep an eye on my nephew and slammed the door on her way out.

I peeled the bloody clothes off, hopped in the shower, put some clothes on and laid on the couch. My nephew will be up soon and I wanted to make sure he knew someone was here. He's been known to try and cook his own eggs.

I laid there thinking about what my mother said and she's right. Menace will kill me and anyone else, without hesitation. Maybe, I should back up. I looked down at my ringing phone and picked it up.

"What?"

"Don't be like that."

"Nigga, you left me and Candy."

"Shut yo whiny ass up and be prepared to take Menace down."

"I'm not doing anything without my cousin. You know, the one who was shot and you left."

"Bitch, you don't have a choice. Now be ready when I call." He hung up. I closed my eyes and tried to figure out, what to do. I damn sure ain't going nowhere with him.

Menace

"So you're telling me, Block told you to come in the club and shoot it up?" I asked the guy we found outside. Had it not been for Valley spotting him out, we wouldn't have never known who he was.

When the waitress came and found us, you could tell how nervous she was. Once she relayed the message, Joakim and I took off. By the time we reached the VIP area, a small explosion had gone off by the door. It wasn't bad and looked more like fireworks than anything. Unfortunately, it caused major chaos and people were everywhere. In the process, Block was able to sneak away but not before Valley shot him. We had people at all the hospitals but he never came. Joakim told me, he looked on the camera and he was hit. Quana's stupid ass and some random people helped him to car, which we found out is Candy's. Valley didn't know but the fact he even got the plate number with everything going on, is impressive.

"Block, told us someone raped his mom and the person was in the club. Look man. We don't even know the dude." I stared at the guy speak and his entire demeanor was off. He was nervous but more about dying then he did, with the lie he spit out. One thing, I can't stand is a fucking liar. It burns me up for someone not to be truthful.

"Who's your family?" Joakim asked and I knew what was coming next and so did everyone else, that's why they were shaking their heads.

"I'm a Thorton, why?" There were a lot of them but one person in the family stood out.

"Are you related to Judge Thorton?" I stood and walked over to him.

"Yea, that's my aunt, why."

"Sucks, she'll have to bury you." I looked at Joakim and he pulled the trigger.

"Make sure when the news hit, we send the family flowers. I want the bitch to know exactly who did it." I hated judge Thorton and had good reason to.

When I left Quana this last time, I ran into her at a store, we exchanged numbers and I hit her off a few times. Now I thought, I'd get lucky like my boy Camari and get a judge who wasn't worried about the system looking at her crazy for dealing with someone like me but no. This bitch wanted to hide out, fuck in different towns and even had the audacity to ask me to take her on vacations.

She was a beautiful woman and would've made a good wife but she worried more about what people would say. Not that she shouldn't, due to her occupation but her job was the least of my worries. She spoke of the white people in the courthouse who stereotyped black people. *A judge and thug won't go together in the eyes of corporate America,* is what she said. I fucked her real good one last time and blocked her. Unfortunately, putting this good dick in her life, turned her into a damn stalker. Even to this very day, the bitch constantly calls me from different numbers and I block each one.

A few of the corner boys got locked up and once she found out they worked for me, she tried to give them hard time. I sent my lawyer in and made sure each one got off. See, shorty

216

has the upper hand on a lotta shit in the court system but I'm the man on the streets and she should know, I'll always have a spade or two hidden. My lawyer and I are tight so he was aware of the text messages, phone calls, explicit photos and videos she sent me. Therefore; it was a no win situation, anytime one of my workers came in and she hated it.

"You cold bro," Joakim put his gun back in his waist.

"Nigga, you pulled the trigger."

"You gave me the signal."

"You were gonna kill him anyway."

"How you know that?"

"Nigga, once you ask who's their family, we all know what's next."

"Hmmm. I have to change that."

"Get the fuck outta here and go see what my sister wants. Got her calling me because yo ass murking motherfuckers."

"Say what you want but when I murk a nigga, she knows how much it bothers me and takes extra special care of a nigga."

217

"Really?" He knew damn well killing doesn't bother him.

"I'm serious. She.-" He was about to say some shit to piss me off. Like any brother; no one wants to hear the shit his sister does in the bedroom. Not that he'd really tell me but he damn sure got a kick outta fucking with me.

"Stop fucking playing."

"See y'all later." He put up the peace sign and walked out. Everyone followed behind but I stayed put. I wanted to make sure the clean-up was done correctly. Mistakes are made too often and I refused to go down for any.

I sat in my chair, took out my laptop and pulled up the cameras where Dynasty and Taylor's shop were going up at. The demolition was done quickly and the building had begun. I had cameras put in across the street on the telephone pole, to make sure everything was getting done and people weren't slacking off. Surprisingly, they were on schedule. The frames were up and you could see the electricians had begun as well because wires were everywhere.

"What you doing here?" I asked Dynasty and leaned back in my chair. She closed the door and locked it. I smirked when she removed the jacket.

"Well, you were at a bachelor party and I know seeing all that scattered ass and rotten coochie probably turned you on."

"How you know its rotten?"

"If its not mine, then its rotten."

"Touché."

"Now, like I was saying. Your dick is probably ready to feel these warm walls around it." She lifted her leg and the heels made her nakedness, even sexier.

"How you know, I didn't handle it already?"

"Because you won't allow another man to touch me and that's what would happen if you cheated on me." I put my hands on her waist and sat her on my desk.

"When you have the best at home, there's no need to look elsewhere." I planted a kiss on her stomach and stood up.

"Make that your last time mentioning another man touching you." I placed my hand behind her neck and made her look at me.

"Menace." She appeared to be frightened. I unbuckled my jeans and let them fall to the floor with my boxers.

"I would never hurt you Dynasty but that's one thing, I'd kill you over."

"I…" She stopped speaking and bit into my shoulder when I forcefully entered her. There was no making love right now and she knew it.

"You are the woman God sent me and I'm not willing to risk anything we have and lose you." I whispered and let my hand go around her throat. Her eyes were closed and I felt her pearl swelling around my dick.

"You like this rough shit Dy?"

"Yesssss." I squeezed a little tighter, maneuvered in and out and her entire body convulsed.

"You so got damn sexy." I stared at her coat my dick.

"I love you baby." She wrapped her arms around my neck and kissed me. I picked her up and thrusted harder.

"I love you too Dy."

The two of us stayed there for a while, moaning out each other's name. When you're in love with someone, the sex is not only mind blowing but will have you on a natural high. I swear, she and I could fuck for hours and I would never get tired of being inside her. For the life of me, I'll never understand how men can have everything at home and still go out to cheat. I guess, temptation is a bitch and it may be true. However, hurting a woman who gives you the world, is fucked up on many levels. I never wanted to see a woman cry over me for that reason.

"What's that?" She pointed to the computer and put the belt around her coat.

"What?"

"That?" She looked closer,

"Nosy." I closed the laptop.

"But if you must know, I brought some land and started building on it."

"That's great Menace. The more businesses you open, the faster you can retire." I looked at her. Quana never once congratulated me on anything or even asked me to leave the street life alone.

"What?"

"Nothing." I pulled her close.

"Would you marry me, if I asked you today?"

"Without hesitation."

"Damn, you are something special." I put my face in the crook of her neck.

"Now, hold on."

"What?"

"I know you have money and a lot of it. I'm not asking for any of it, or special favors."

"Spit it out babe."

"Ummm, I can't marry you and live in that house. I mean, it's a gorgeous but I refuse to build memories in a place you spent with another woman. Bad enough, I've been laying in the same bed."

"You can have whatever you want Dy."

"I want you, our baby and whatever you want."

"Look for a spot. You can buy a house or have one built from the ground up. Tell me when you find it so I can buy it." She was about to protest.

"I know you have money. You brought a house and gave your mom some. Save the rest and let me take care of you. I don't mind and I don't want you to think I'm trying to buy you."

"You do know, I spend a lot of money in K-Mart, and Express." I tossed my head back laughing. That's nothing compared to what Quana used to spend.

"Baby, you can spend all my money in the dollar store if you wanted."

"Don't tempt me. They have nice stuff in there." I grabbed her hand, turned the lights off and locked up.

"Why is he here cleaning so late?"

"We had to handle business." She stared at me.

"You better not had let the strippers come here and have sex on the floor."

"Hell no! The only stripper coming here, is walking out the door with me."

223

"You damn right." She did a twerking dance in front of me and I stopped.

"You been holding out."

"I just learned how to do it."

"It looks good too." I smacked her ass and walked her to her car.

"I'll see you at home."

"I'm right behind you." I closed her door and she waited for me to get in my truck. The little things like this made me fall deeper in love with her. How many women you know wait for their man? Shit, she better hope I don't drag her ass to the courthouse in the morning and really take her up on marrying me.

****

"You ready?" I asked Dynasty who was coming down the steps looking tired as hell. She was up half the night with morning sickness.

"Yea. Lets get this over with."

"You better not let Jen hear you speak like that." I was dropping her off at the hotel. Jen and Valley were getting

224

married tomorrow and she wanted her bridal party to stay the night with her.

"I know. Baby, can you grab my bag?"

"I put it in the truck already with your dress." She smiled.

"Thanks and can we stop at Dunkin donuts?"

"You want coffee this late?"

"I want a tea. I think it will settle my stomach."

"If you took the anti-nausea pill the doctor gave you, this wouldn't be happening." She stuck her finger up but it was true. The doctor told her to take it regardless if she felt good or not and she missed it one day and look what happened.

"I took it today and I brought it with me."

"Good. I don't need my woman looking shitty in the wedding photos."

"Really?"

"Yup. I swear, you'll be standing alone." Her mouth fell open and I laughed.

"Come on with your stubborn ass." I pressed the alarm on the car and got in.

"What's that?" She pointed to a piece of paper on the windshield. I took it off and sat back in the car.

You're going to get what's coming to you for hurting me and others around. You won't get away with this.

"Who is that from?"

"Probably Quana. I'll handle it."

"You think she'll come after me? I'm not scared but I am for the baby."

"She's not crazy. Don't worry about anything. I got you."

"Menace, I'm not coming here when the wedding's over. We can stay at my place or even a hotel." I nodded because I understood the way she felt and she had every right to feel the way she did. The bitch came to the house while we here, which means she's not only bold but testing the fuck outta me. I see its time to make a stop at her house.

Jen

"I'll see you at the altar baby." Valley was about to leave and go to the hotel. They were staying in the one across the street from us. He didn't want anything to happen and he couldn't get to me.

"Valley, I have something to tell you." My hands were sweaty and even though I should've told him sooner, the shit was eating me up.

"What?" He stood at the door.

"I don't know how to tell you this but…" His phone started vibrating on his waist. He never looked down and kept his eyes on me.

"Say it."

"Huh?"

"Say it." I didn't like the way he said it. Did he know already? Why was he looking at me like that?

"Ummm. Well a long time ago." His phone vibrated again and he still didn't remove his gaze from me.

"Why are you hesitating? It can't be that bad."

227

"It sorta is."

"Oh yea." He put his bag down and folded his arms across his chest.

"A long time ago, I…" The tears started falling down my face and he moved closer to me.

"If it makes you this upset, don't say it. I don't want you hurting in any way. Our wedding is all you've talked about and I want it to be as special as, you made it."

"But…" He grabbed my face and put both hands on the side.

"But nothing. I'm sure whatever it is, I already know." He had a sad look on his face and placed a kiss on my lips.

"Valley." He picked his bag up and turned around.

"Jen, go have fun and stop worrying about irrelevant things. When I say, your man got you. I really got you." I ran over and hugged him tight.

"Nothing and I mean nothing is going to stop me from making you my wife. Do you hear me?" I nodded my head.

"I love you Jen and tomorrow you will be my wife, come hell or high water."

"I'm sorry."

"I know baby. I know." He kissed my lips and shut the door behind him. I stood there staring at it. I wanted to run after him and tell him so it wasn't a secret but he refused to let me. I wonder if he knew and didn't wanna deal with it. I went upstairs, grabbed my things and drove over to the hotel.

"Yea baby." I called him when I got there like he asked. "I'm here."

"Ok. Have fun and stop worrying."

"Are you gonna meet me at the altar? Please tell me now. I don't wanna be the bride who got stood up."

"Like I said before. Nothing is going to stop me from making you my wife."

"Ok. I love you."

"I love you too." I hung up and blew my breath out. I hope he meant what he said because if he left me at the altar, I'll fucking kill him.

****

"You look beautiful Jen." Taylor came out the bathroom in her dress and sat next to me.

229

"He's not going to leave you at the altar. Shit, as late as we are, he probably thinks you won't show." We were already forty minutes late and Menace called Dynasty to ask where we were. Talking about they tired of standing there.

"I'm scared. What if he pulls a tape out or says I don't want this bitch, in front of everyone. Fuck this, I'm not going."

WHAP! Dynasty smacked the shit outta me.

"Calm the fuck down and put the dress back on. You're panicking for nothing."

"Really?"

"Yes, fucking really. If he didn't wanna marry you, he wouldn't go through all this. Menace told me, he is excited and couldn't wait to make you his wife. Now come on because I'm hungry." Taylor started laughing. I grabbed the dress, put it back on and had the makeup chick fix me up. I was so nervous and crying, I messed it up.

"About time." Taylor and Dynasty both shouted when I came out the room.

"Let's go. I told Joakim we were on the way ten minutes ago and the church is only five minutes away. He's

230

gonna curse me out for lying." I waved her off and we left the room and stepped on the elevator.

"Somethings not right." Dynasty said and peeked out the elevator before any of us got off.

"Here she go with that intuition shit." Taylor moved past her and stopped dead in her tracks.

"Now what?"

"He's here." She tried to step back on the elevator.

"Who?"

"Donnell. I swear, he walked past the hotel. Look." She pointed and no one was there when we looked outside.

"Girl, let's get in the limo before they send a search party for us." Taylor peeked out the door and basically ran to it. Dynasty waited for me to get in and sat on the opposite side.

"Are you ready?" Taylor was still looking out the back window. Whoever she saw may have resembled Donnell but why would he be here? And how would he even know she was here? The driver pulled up to the church and we hurried to get out.

"Got dammit!" Dynasty yelled as we walked to the front of the church.

"Girl, you going to hell for cursing in the church."

"I have a pain in my leg." She opened the door and the rest of the bridal party was waiting. I had them leave earlier to show Valley, I was on my way.

"You ok?"

"I guess." She stood and fatigue washed her over.

"You sure, you're ok?"

"I'm fine. Its my turn to walk." She went ahead and limped a little.

"Where the fuck is Taylor?" I asked and one person said she walked ahead of Dynasty but I didn't see her. Once the music started, the doors re opened and I made my way down the aisle. I could see people smiling and taking pictures. The moment my eyes laid on Valley, it was like I fell in love all over again. I noticed the tears he tried to wipe away before I got there.

"Where's Taylor?" I asked Joakim who shrugged his shoulders and looked behind me. I turned to hand my bouquet to Dynasty and she looked like she was about to pass out. I asked if she wanted to sit but she said no. Her forehead was sweating and everything. Menace didn't agree with her standing either and tried to make her sit but she refused.

"We are gathered here today.-"

BOOM! I heard and turned around. Dynasty was on the floor foaming at the mouth. Menace ran over to her and yelled out for someone to call 911. How the hell is Taylor missing, and my maid of honor is passed out on the floor. Could anything else go wrong?

"HOLD THE FUCK UP! YOU'RE NOT MARRYING HER BECAUSE SHE'S MY BITCH!" Someone shouted and the blood drained from my face. He had Taylor in front of him with a machete around her neck.

"WHAT THE FUCK?" Joakim barked and headed towards Taylor. When I saw who came in and stood next to him, everything started to come together.

TO BE CONTINUED...

Made in the USA
Columbia, SC
06 March 2018